Lock Down Publications and Ca$h
Presents

I0666811

TIPPIN' THE
SCALES
HIGHWAY KINGPINS

Written By
Christopher "Diesel" Hornezes

CHRISTOPHER "DIESEL" HORNEZES

First Edition 2025

Printed in the United States of America

This is a work of fiction. Names, characters, places, and incidents either
are products of the author's imagination or are used fictitiously. Any
similarity to actual events or locales or persons, living or dead, is
entirely coincidental.

Lock Down Publications
P.O. Box 944
Stockbridge, GA 30281
www.lockdownpublications.com

Like our page on Facebook: Lock Down Publications
www.facebook.com/lockdownpublications.ldp

Stay Connected with Us!

Text **LOCKDOWN** to 22828 to stay up-to-date with new releases, sneak peaks, contests and more…

Like our page on Facebook:
Lock Down Publications

Join Lock Down Publications/The New Era Reading Group

Visit our website:
www.lockdownpublications.com

Follow us on Instagram:
Lock Down Publications

Email Us: We want to hear from you!

PROLOGUE

"Hey," the hefty Mexican security guard shouted at a girl crouching next to one of the semi-trucks he and his crew oversaw. "This is private property! What are you doing over here?"

It was just after 2 o'clock on a Saturday morning in Antioch, Illinois. He and his men had been snorting lines of cocaine, some snorting crystal meth, and drinking. He was wired and ready for some action. As he'd been doing a routine walk-around, the specially trained 95-pound male German Shepherd dog had alerted to something. His ears pricked up as he heard tinkering.

The guard allowed the dog to pull him in the direction that the sound was coming from and as he hurried along the front side of a row of brand new day-cab style semi-tractors, that sat in the huge truck parking section lot of Fast Lane Logistics, owned by Victor Gomez, prince of the infamous Rojas-Gomez cartel, the guard and his dog stumbled upon the girl.

The German Shepherd barked and growled viciously at the girl, raring to be let go to rip her to pieces. With his flashlight in his hand, the guard shined his light on her and did a quick visual check.

She looked to be about 5'5". She was garbed in a baggy black hoodie, black leggings that showed off her shapely bottom half, and on her feet were black Timberlands. Shining the light on her face, he could see her brown eyes and her brown-sugar face. Her long hair was braided back into neat cornrows, the tails hanging down past her chest. What he couldn't see was from her nose down, due to the black bandana she was wearing that had skeleton teeth prints over where her mouth was.

"Um... I was checkin' my tire pressure," she told him.

The guard's eyebrow rose up. "First, take that goddamn mask off," he demanded, his hand now resting on the butt of his holstered semi-automatic 9mm.

The girl complied. Immediately, the guard faltered. She was so gorgeous that he almost started swooning over her. She had the most exotic-looking face and, for a second, he was lost in a trance, until his dog's barking brought him back to reality.

"You are *not* a driver here! Tell me what the fuck you're doing on this property, or I *will* let my dog get you!"

For emphasis, he let two inches of the dog's leash go. The German Shepherd lurched forward, coming to just within a few inches of her. The dog was so close that she could feel the heat coming from his barking.

The girl didn't even blink; instead, she started smirking at the guard.

"Aight. Okay," she then said. "You wanna' know why I'm here for real, right?"

Hearing her speak more clearly as herself, the guard heard what sounded like a New York-like accent.

"Yes! Now! Or you'll be dog food!"

She grinned demonically, then she put two fingers at her lips and gave a loud whistle.

For a second, the guard's eyebrows furrowed at why she'd done that, until two massive dogs came from seemingly out of nowhere and bum-rushed *his* dog. The two smacked into the German Shepherd like Great White Sharks ascending from the depths of the ocean, after locking in on an unsuspecting seal, floating on the surface.

The German Shepherd's cries made the guard wince. Frozen in shock, he could do nothing but watch what looked

5

like two huge black and brown tiger-striped Pit Bulls tore his dog up.

"S-s-stop them! Call them off!" he nearly begged, hand struggling to pop the strap that kept his gun in the holster.

The girl started laughing. "How about... *no.*"

The bigger of the two demon dogs sank his teeth into the German Shepherd's muzzle, chomping down with amazing power, and locking his jaws. With one hard tug, the German Shepherd's snout was ripped clean off.

"*Noooo! Soto!*" the guard shouted as the smaller female ripped the right side of his guard dog's face off.

He unstrapped his gun and went to pull it out, ready to blast the girl, who was still just standing there, laughing at him.

"*You bitch! You're gonna die!*" he yelled.

Before he could get his gun out, he heard a gun cocking, then felt the kiss of a barrel on the back of his head.

"Ah ah aahh... bitch-nigga I would *not* do that."

Hearing a male's voice behind him, the guard immediately knew he was screwed.

"Bae, take his gun," the man behind him said, as the two Cane Corsos finished the German Shepherd off.

The guard stood still as the girl complied with her man's directive. She held it up, then called her dogs off the dead guard dog.

"W-Who are y-y-you?" the guard asked as the girl stepped back, cocking his pistol.

The man who had him stuck finally walked into his line of sight. Unlike the woman, the guy wasn't wearing a mask, and he was holding a gun that looked like it should be mounted on the roof of a military Humvee, equipped with a big ammunition box.

He was much taller than the girl, 5'11, he supposed, and despite the baggy black hoodie, jeans, and Timberlands, he could tell the man was in great shape. He had a golden-brown skin tone, long braids, with a very sharp beard and baby hairline. What the guard noticed most, was his green eyes that were like emeralds.

"We are the people your boss keeps fucking with," the girl spoke, as the two big dogs stood at her side, their eyes on the guard, their muzzles smeared with the blood of *his* dog.

"And," the man chimed in, "*we* the ones who gon' show dude that he fuckin' with the *wrong* ones."

Green eyes grabbed the guard's radio and then looked at him. His woman raised the 9mm up, pointing at the guard's face.

"Call your men, tell them to come quick… intruder alert," green eyes told the guard.

Scared shitless, the guard did as told when green eyes pushed the talk button down. A frantic reply from one of the guard's subordinates came, asking what his 20 was. The guard told him in front of the new trucks.

Green eyes dropped the radio and crushed it under his boot. His woman hurried to grab her weapon of choice from her duffle bag. The guard's bladder released when he saw her pull out a machete.

Green eyes saw the guard's men burst out of the office seconds later. He smirked to himself, then he and his woman ducked in between the trucks and waited.

***

"*¡Alla!*" yelled one of the guards, seeing where his and the eleven other security guards' boss stood, in the middle of the bright light. "*¡Vamanos!*" he commanded.

All of them equipped with assault rifles and back-up pistols, ran to assist their boss. They saw him waving his hands frantically, hearing him shout. They were so focused on getting to him, that it wasn't until they were just about 20 feet away that they heard him yelling, "*Nooo! It's a trap!!*"

They then saw a man hop out from in between two trucks with a huge gun. A few of them skidded on the asphalt, trying to stop and change direction, while the others tried to take aim and start firing first.

BRRRRRRRRRRRRRRRRRRRRRRRR!

The big automatic gun let loose, sending a hailstorm of .5.56mm rounds flying at them like swarms of angry bees.

Bullets hit the guards, making them dance like they were on Broadway. Body parts flew off in every direction; heads exploded like dynamite had been implanted inside of their skulls and set off. Bodies hit the ground, looking like bloody meat after a cow got hacked up.

In mere seconds, the head security guards' men were dead, scattered all around, looking like the bloody battleground of Gettysburg. His bowels let loose, and he filled his underwear up to the point that it pushed out and started running down his legs.

Green eyes stopped firing when all the guards were in pieces. He turned back and looked at the head guard, seeing that the man was trembling in fear. He chuckled at the guy, walking up to him.

"¿Que paso, 'mano? You look scared right now," he said, then a light breeze blew in his direction, carrying the foul odor in the man's briefs. "Damn!" he said, waving a hand in front of his nose. "Scared shitless, should I say?" he teased.

"P-P-Please! I just work here, man," the guard begged.

Green eyes looked at where his woman stood a few feet behind the man, holding her machete. Their dogs stood by her side, waiting for a command. To his woman, green eyes nodded his head. The girl winded up like she was about to hit a home run. The guard peeped the nod and spun around to see the girl.

"Wait! Nooo!" he screamed as she swung the machete.

THWACK!

The blade sliced right through his thigh, severing his whole leg. The guard fell to the ground, screaming in agony as blood spurted from the stump.

"Eat," the girl told her dogs.

Immediately, the two ran to the severed leg and started tearing into it, like hungry Hyenas on a fresh Caribou hindquarter.

The guard cried his eyes out as the pain grew to be unbearable. Green eyes and his woman stepped up, standing over the guard.

He looked up at them and shitted on himself even more.

"You picked the wrong one to work for, my man," said green eyes, "and now, you will pay for it with your life."

The guard then saw the woman raise the machete up high over her head. Before she brought it back down, he closed his eyes and prayed to the Lord for forgiveness, pleading to let him through those pearly gates, because he was on the way.

WHACK!

"One more thing to do, guapo," the girl told her man, pulling the machete out of the middle of the guard's sliced face.

"Yep," Green eyes agreed, then walking back out to the middle of the yard, he raised up the barrel of his M249 and squeezed the trigger.

The girl watched her man blow slugs at every truck and trailer, destroying them effortlessly. He turned the gun and blew at the building, putting so many holes in it that the roof collapsed.

She then raised up the hem of her hoodie, revealing a utility belt with incendiary grenades clipped onto it. She unclipped one, pulled the pin, and tossed it at a row of trucks. It exploded, creating a massive fireball that started burning what could've been repaired.

She did the same with the rest of her grenades. Once all ten of them were used, the entire yard was on fire. Tens of millions of dollars worth of equipment had been destroyed in less than ten minutes.

"Mission accomplished, baby," said green eyes, delighted by all the blazes he was looking at like a pyromaniac. "I can't *wait* for Mister *Bitch*-tor Gomez to figure out who did this," he said, as they and their dog hurried off, running towards the rear fence where he'd cut a hole into it.

"You know Danny and ChaCha are gonna' hear about it, too, though, right?" his woman asked, as they reached the fence.

"Why you gotta kill the mode, bae?" He opened the hole up wide for her and their dog to go through, then squeezed out behind them.

"I'm just sayin', papi. Better be prepared. They're gonna be pissed."

"¡Que se joda! Dude blew up three of *my* trucks last week, so I blew up fifty of *his*!"

His girl started laughing as they ran through the dark wooded area that was behind the yard. They got to where the stolen black 1999 BMW 750i sat idling in a deep cut off the side of Route 173 and hopped in.

Behind the wheel, the girl slammed it in drive and mashed the gas, making the V12 engine lurch them forward out of the spot and rocket them east, hurrying to get far away from the carnage they created.

"What's next, amor?" he asked his woman, as he wiped their dog's bloody snout with a baby wipe.

"I gotta handle this crooked-ass lawyer in Waukegan, then I have a crooked, racist-ass human trafficking Texas State Trooper to handle," she told him.

"Damn, man. I wish you were riding with me out to Jersey," he said, tossing the wet wipe out of the window.

"When I get back, we'll have all the time we need to ourselves, but business comes first," she said, as Lake County Sheriff's cars flew past them, heading towards the raging inferno that *was* Fast Lane Logistics. "I'ma tell you this, though," she said, her tone of voice going from business, to serious, as she turned and faced him, just as she reached the Route 173 and Interstate 94 junction. "If I hear you went around that fucking traga bitch while I'm out of town, ¡Te lo juro por *fucking* Dios, la voy a cortar en pedazos a esa *puta* y se la alimento a Demon y Diamond! ¿Me entiendes?

Javi's heart damn nearly dropped out of his chest at the sudden change in conversation. He glanced over at her and saw the fire in her eyes.

"Y-Yo no se quien hablas," he capped, stammering and looking away from her.

"Uh-huh. You *know* who I'm talking about. Play stupid. You gon' get her ass turned into ground *bitch*! Try me if you want to!"

He swallowed hard then. He knew his woman was *not* playing. She'd done it before, with one of his other honey dips.

Chapter 1
Stacks

Late Spring, 2015
4 Days Later... Downtown Waukegan, Illinois.
It was three o'clock in the morning when the front doors of the Lake County Jail opened, releasing a demon back onto the streets. The 6'0 tall man was dark-skinned, with an athletic build, sporting a bald-fade haircut, with waves up top. His beard needed a trim and a lineup, but sitting in jail for the last month, fighting firearm possession charges kept him from being able to maintain himself the way he would on the outs.

Stacks was from out west in Chicago, raised in the K-Town neighborhood. He was an *Unknown Vicelord*; a red 5-point star was tatted over his Adam's apple, and a reaper in a red hoodie was inked on his left forearm. He was still with the nation shit but was about money more than anything. At 26 years old, he was on some grown-man shit, and to be on it, he needed grown-man money. His pockets were empty. He wasn't having that.

He *hated* Lake County with a passion. He'd only left *Chiraq* to come stain all the wannabe dope boys and dope girls he'd always heard other Chi-Town goons had come up to hit licks on but had ended up living in North Chicago, a.k.a. *Nogo*, for the last five years. His right-hand man had made the trip up from the city with him. Together, the two

Ghosts had hit many licks and had come up substantially. But neither of them would be happy until they were rich.

During his time up in *Nogo*, and *Wauk-Town*, Stacks had bumped a lot of women. The ladies of Lake County loved the Chicago gangsters. He ended up getting two pregnant, and had a daughter, and a son. He regretted getting his daughter's mother pregnant every day of his life since he'd found out about the redhead's bodily issues. The pussy and head were so fire that he didn't care, until the true nature of her problem was revealed, in a crowded public setting. He was *repulsed* by her. To the current day, Stacks still tried to use her for certain things for his own gain, but she had fallen way back off him. And it had Stacks seeing *red*.

Finally free after the month-long visit, of which Stacks was sure he would be seeing NRC Statesville once again, he was already plotting his comeback. He learned valuable information while inside and couldn't wait to tell his homeboy.

Rocking the True Religion sweat suit and Air Jordan 5s he'd gotten arrested in, Stacks stood outside of the jail's entrance. Beyond the entrance to the construction zone for the $100 million dollar courthouse that was being added to the Lake County judicial system, he saw the crooked attorney's office building that had been burned a few days ago.

While he was on the unit inside, he and a bunch of other detainees were at the window, when the flames shot out of the corner building's windows. Crowds of people surrounded the office building while firefighters fought to extinguish the flames. After the fire was out, the attorney and his secretary were discovered, charred beyond recognition.

Everyone was geeked that someone finally got at the corrupt lawyer. He'd been stealing clients' money, blowing off court dates, taking bogus plea deals instead of fighting, and spent most of his time snorting cocaine in his office, fucking whores that he got released from jail, accepting pussy and head as payment.

Stacks crossed the street and entered a small parking lot where a little fast-food shack was. He waited for ten more minutes before he got even angrier.

"I *knew* this bitch wasn't gon' be here, joe! I'ma smack the fuck out that bitch! On the *Five!*" he growled.

Stacks knew of a McDonalds that was always open. It was a ten-minute walk from where he was. He got to strolling, walking north up, coming to the corner of County and Washington, where the charred attorney's office was, he banged a right onto Washington, shooting down to Genesee, then went left. Walking past all the businesses that lined both sides of the street, Stacks continued to put together a plan that could have him pushing a new Bentley and living in a mansion.

He got to Grand Avenue minutes after passing the big Genesee theatre and hit a right, crossing the street with his eyes set on the McDonalds. As he got closer, he saw a bummy-looking man yelling at someone on the phone. He was accompanied by an even rattier-looking woman.

"Aye!" Stacks hollered to the man. "Aye, Famo'!"

The guy and his woman paused, seeing Stacks walking towards them.

"What up, fam? Aye? You got some hard on you, my nigga?" the guy asked, with wide eyes that displayed that he was fiending for crack.

CRACK!

Without any warning, Stacks cocked back and socked the man in his jaw, knocking him clean out.

The woman screamed, *"Hey! What the hell, dude?!"*

SMACK!

"Shut up, bitch," said Stacks after he gave her an open-hand smack that made her take off running, leaving her clucker boyfriend sleeping on the concrete.

Stacks snatched the man's phone from the ground where it landed, then he went into the cluck's pockets and found $60 dollars.

"Good lookin' out, joe," he said, then hurried off before anybody started getting nosey.

Bending the corner from Grand, back onto Genesee Street, Stacks dialed his daughter's mother's phone as he walked towards Waukegan's infamous *Tower* apartment building.

No answer.

"Bitch," he cursed, getting even angrier that she'd told him that she would come get him, then not even answer her phone when he called to see where the fuck she was at. "Bet money her ass got a dick in her mouth right now," he told himself, dialing another number.

He got an answer in three rings.

"Who the hell is this callin' me so late?" Jasmine snapped.

"It's me. I finna come over there."

"Dontae?" she asked.

"Yeah, bitch! Duh! Who the fuck else gon' call yo' ass 'n say that?! You got another dude or somethin'?"

"No! I thought yo' ass was still locked up, though!"

"They dropped my case. I woulda' got out earlier but I got into it with the police, so they made me wait 'til midnight to get booked out."

"You want me to come get you?" Jasmine asked.

"Naw. Kenzie was supposed to, but her ass sent me off. I'ma beat the fuck out her ass when I catch her."

"Fuck that shitty-booty-ass slut. I'll come get you, bae."

"Naw. I know my son sleep. I'ma get Rambo to come get me. I'll be there soon, aight?"

"Yeah. Love you, baby."

"Yo ass better. Love you, too."

Stacks reached the Towers and called his Ghost homie Rambo.

Rambo answered on the second ring. "Fuck is this?"

15

"Me, nigga! I need a ride to Jas's crib."

"Oh shit! My nigga! You got out?"

"Duh! I'm walkin' towards the Towers right now, Lord."

"Aight. I'm on the way. I got some fi-ass tree, too, joe! On Vicelord! You tryna' blow one?"

"I'm always tryna blow. Aye, I got a couple moves for us, too. Hurry up so I can lay 'em on you, bruh."

"Say less. I need some money. On Ghost."

Rambo ended the call then. Stacks posted up outside of the tall building and waited for his homie to come out. He sent a text to another person while he waited.

Aye, shortie it's me. I'm out and I got a dig for us. Be available real soon.

Stacks sent the message and started thinking about all the other licks he and his goon squad could hit. The best ones seemed like a cartel stash house, and a family of truck-driving Dominicans that supposedly brought in *tons* of cocaine, flooding the whole Midwest with supreme product. He only hoped he could find a way to get locations, so he and his crew could make it happen.

Chapter 2
JAVI

Out in Gurnee

"*Ooooo!* ¡Ay, Dios *mio*, Jabier!" The thick 5'4" peanut-butter-toned Puerto Rican chick, as Javi pounded her from the back, as Wisin y Yandel's *Rakata* bumped from the surround-sound speakers wired up in her deluxe bedroom. He long stroked her soaking wet pussy while her long black hair was wrapped around his hand. "¡Chacho, papi! I no can take it! *¡Coño!*" she cried out, feeling herself ready to cum again, for the fourth time.

Javi gritted his teeth and fucked her even faster, harder, putting all nine inside her. Her fat, round, 48-inch ass looked so good when it jiggled every time he went in. She was ass-naked, on all fours on her bed, with only red Jimmy Choo stilettos on her feet. Face down, ass up, Javi dominated the Boricua beauty, just like she liked for him to do.

"*Fuck!*" he shouted as the tight wetness of her overwhelmed his loins. "*¡Cono!* This pussy is so good!"

Angela was ecstatic to hear how much her pussy had him going crazy. All she wanted was to please him. The 23-year-old was originally from Puerto Rico. She migrated to Miami when she was grown enough to leave the nest. Having gotten a taste of the fast life in her mid-teens, she instantly got into it. Exotic dancing: shaking her ass for cash and fucking whatever baller had the biggest bankroll.

A year later, Angela made the mistake of hitting a lick on a kingpin and had to flee Miami. She found herself in Illinois, dancing at a well-known club where Chi-Town's wealthiest elite underworld bosses went to blow off steam. She met Javi there and instantly fell in love with his green eyes.

His diamond jewelry, his expensive clothing, and his handsome GQ looks had him barely having to say hello before he had her in the back of his Rolls-Royce sucking his dick. After he dicked her down, she was his. At least, she *thought* she was.

For the last year and a half, Javi had been fucking Angela. During that time, she discovered that he had a woman, who he was crazy in love with. It fucked her up, but she decided to play her role in hopes of him one day seeing *her* as *wifey* instead of pussy. She did everything he wanted. Sucked him, fucked him, and cooked for him. She was such a skilled chef that Javi bought her a restaurant and even put it in her name. He also bought the big luxurious 4,600-square-foot 3-story house she lived in, along with the new SRT-8 Jeep Cherokee, and the new Porsche Cayenne Turbo.

Angela was completely gone over the 24-year-old boss. She wanted him for herself so badly. She knew the only way to make that happen was to get his woman out of the way.

"¡Aayyyy, Javier!" she cried out again, lifting her head up as she came closer to cumming. "¡Te amo, papi! ¡Yo te *fucking* amo!"

Javi *never* said he loved her back. He loved the *pussy*, but not *her*. She was his honey-dip, a jump-off. He had a woman that he loved and not just fucked but made love to. Angela was just a thot that he used to get a nut off. Despite it, though, Javi didn't mind spoiling the bitch. He hit her off with cash and bought her things, and when he bought her the restaurant, Javi had seen it as an opportunity to bring in more money. So, he invested in her for a percentage of her earnings.

Javi went savage on her, hitting hit hard and fast from the back until she exploded, cumming all over his dick. He kept her on all fours, pulling his wet dick out of her. Angela laid her face down on her bed, reached her hands back, and gripped her sweaty ass cheeks, opening them up for him. Javi spit a wad of saliva into her crack, right on her puckered-up asshole, then with the bulbous tip of his dick, he smeared his spit all over her chute, getting it nice and wet for him to slide up in it.

Javi entered her tight asshole as Don Omar and Tego Calderon's *Bandalero* came on.

Angela hissed as she felt him entering her. He eased himself in, careful not to hurt her. Once she got used to his tool inside, Angela turned up her freak mode, demanding him to turn up as well.

"¡Meteme ese bicho, Javier! ¡Dámelo *duro*! ¡Dámelo!" she moaned out, begging him for that savage dick while she tooted her ass up as high as she could for him.

Javi fucked her like the slut she wanted to be for him. He hit it hard, smacked her ass, pulled her hair, all while he talked dirty to her.

"¡Dime cuánto te encanta este bicho, puta!" he asked her, wanting her to tell him how much she liked the dick.

"¡Aaay, yeess papi! ¡Me encanta!" she screamed out at the tops of her lungs.

Angela squealed as she felt Javi's dick in her asshole going all the way in and out of her. She clenched her anal tract tightly around him, adding to the friction he already felt. She wanted to make him cum *hard*. Seconds later, she exploded again, so hard that she nearly passed out.

Javi cursed and groaned as he felt his nuts tightening up. His back muscles got tight, and he could feel his nut coming. Angela felt his dick swelling up in her asshole. She knew he was less than a minute away from cumming.

She quickly took him out of her ass, pushed him off the bed onto his feet, and dropped down before him on her knees. She opened wide for him to put his dick back into her mouth while she looked up at him.

"¡*Mama*melo este bicho, puta!" Javi demanded as she took his dick and put it into her mouth. "Suck this muhfucka and swallow *all* this *dulce de leche,* bitch!"

Angela sucked and jerked Javi until he exploded. He roared animalistically as he skeeted in her mouth. He grabbed her head and fucked her face until he was empty and her mouth was full of semen. Putting on a show for him, Angela opened her mouth and let it dribble out, spilling onto her succulent 36DD-cup breasts.

"Mmmm, papi, I *lobe* the way you taste," she said.

Javi chuckled at her. He loved how her accent was so strong that whenever she said his name or a word in English that had a '*V*', she pronounced it like it was a '*B*'. That was because in Spanish, '*V*' and '*B*' made the same sound.

"Yeah? You love it, huh?"

Angela nodded. "Si, papi. Me haces sentir muy bien." She took Javi's softening dick and kissed the tip of it. "La forma en que me chicha, me encanta mucho."

"I know I make you feel good, and I know you love the way I fuck you." He took her by the hand and pulled her up off her knees, just as Lil' Durk's *Like Me* featuring Jeremih came on. "My sex game always gon' be official, as long as you keep bein' the lil' nasty freak you are. ¿Me entiende, mamita?" he asked.

"Yes, papi. I understand. I always be your bellaca. Pa' mi, eres el mejor."

"If I'm the best, then go make me some food while I get in the shower. I gotta head off to work soon."

Angela smiled, happy at another chance to impress him. "Lo que tu diga, mi amor," she told him.

Ass naked with her stilettos on, she planned to go cook for him. Javi gave her big booty a slap as she left, and then he grabbed his duffel bag with clean clothes in it before heading to her bathroom to get showered.

After a hot shower, Javi dressed in a tight black V-neck t-shirt, with 501 Levi's jeans, and his black Timberlands. He put his long white-gold Cuban link chain on and then donned the white-gold Cartier.

In the full-body mirror in Angela's exclusive bathroom, he checked himself, nodding in approval. He stood an athletic 5'11", with rich golden-brown skin, tatted up like Wiz Khalifa. The tails of his long Iverson-style braids hung down his chest; his baby hairline and beard were trimmed and lined so sharply that they looked tattooed on. His green eyes made women swoon over them. They were like emeralds that sparkled.

He was a devilishly handsome young man with tens of millions in multiple offshore and private bank accounts. He'd been putting in work for his family since before he was even a teenager. He'd sold coke, banged hammers, and rid his family of competition. For a pretty boy, as some saw him as, Javi was a certified goon. He wore that title proudly.

"You are a handsome ass *tiguere*, Javier," he told himself, giving his reflection a wink. "Who fuckin' with you, papi? *Nobody!*"

Fresh and clean, Javi got out of the shower and gave himself a fresh beard trim and line-up. He checked himself out in a tall, full-length mirror, nodding in approval of the handsome golden-brown complexioned man that he saw.

As the oldest of three, Javi had a lot of responsibilities. He and his brother and sister were all born and raised in Illinois' Waukegan Township, a northeastern Lake County suburb about forty-odd minutes north of Chicago. It went *down* in Wauk-Town. Gangbanging, drug dealing, cartels, dirty and corrupt trigger-happy cops all made up the infamous suburban town's dark side. Since he was a youngster, Javi had been groomed his father, Ricardo, and his mother Roselyn. Ricardo passed down the game *he'd* been taught by *his* father, Diego, and his uncle's, Pedro and

Juanito. When he jumped off the porch in his early teens, Javi was ready for the world.

***

The Valdez family's multi-billion dollar empire had been created by the three ol' heads of the family, Pedro, Juanito, and Diego, back in the early 70's. Pedro wanted to get rich and decided to get his little brothers on board with the idea of using the acres of farmland in Santo Domingo's Capotlillo neighborhood, in the Dominican Republic, that had been in their family forever, to grow cocaine on. Always having had love and respect for their big bro, Juanito and Diego were down to ride. So, they started growing, and as their cash crops grew, they learned how to do their own cutting and processing. With them, a few close friends that assisted them in the process of turning the plants into cocaine. The day they made their first sale in their neighborhood, word got out that they had that Payow!

Months after being in business, their money was up, and Pedro was wanted to take their product to the United States. His brothers were a little skeptical of that, though. They knew about all the regulations and all the law enforcement agencies that ran the country, and they knew the problems they'd encounter if they got caught. Pedro took a trip out to New York to meet a few friends that had migrated there and set up their own businesses.

He was introduced to some high-powered people, of whom he greased greedy palms of to buy windows of opportunity.

It was on then. Before the trio made their move to the state, Pedro and his brothers sat and got positions established. Pedro would handle the clients; Juanito, having always been a lover of big trucks, was to build a trucking company so that he could get their product shipped around to customers without having to hire middle men; Diego, who

22

had always been rowdy, was charged with building an army, which was right up his alley since he had a best friend that was a native of near-by Kingston, that loved action as well.

The Valdez brothers entered the U.S. and made their names ring bells instantly. They made friends and they made enemies. Their army handled the opps, while Juanito and his few trusted trucker buddies got their coke delivered to their clients. Pedro traveled all around the country with a squad of Caribbean goons as security, scoring new business damn near every day.

For decades, the brothers raked in hundreds of millions of dollars, which turned into billions. Every chance they got, they invested and built more companies, cleaning up their money and building wealth that nobody could touch. Their first priorities were securing futures for their children, their children's children, and so on. The three married their childhood sweethearts and each had a son.

Juanito and Carolina had their son Tomás first; Diego and Maritza had their son Ricardo next, and last, Pedro and Larissa had their son Daniel.

They taught their sons the game and instilled in them the values of a broke man that appreciated every crumb of bread he found, while teaching them how to be smart and how to make money off money that made money.

As the boys grew older, their positions became clear. Tomas was the head honcho, while Ricardo was the goon, and Danny was the truck lover. Together, the three were given major roles in the family's empire, and as easy as pie, they doubled and tripled their family's worth. They put on more family and close friends, making sure that everyone ate, without wanting anything in return. They did things for people out of the kindness of their hearts, but those that opposed them, learned that they would never hesitate to boot up and come gunning for anyone.

In the early 2000s, the Valdez family lost Pedro, after he lost a battle to brain cancer. So many people attended his funeral that one would think that Biggie Smalls and 2Pac were both laid out there. Pedro was a man that was loved by hundreds of people. Danny and his mother Maritza were the most devastated by the loss, but they were also the ones that made sure that the legacy of Pedro Valdez would live on forever.

The family continued, getting money, creating more and more opportunities for people that were not fortunate enough to have the blessings that they did. The Valdezes were very different from other drug-trafficking families. They showed real love, and helped people, even those that weren't even in the game. The one thing the three cousins lived by, taught to them by their fathers, was that bestowing blessing upon people should not be done to receive blessings back. They should be done because they were blessed enough to do it.

Tomas and his Puerto Rican college brainiac, Cristina, had their own two sons, Macho and Tool when they were just shy of 20 years old. Ricardo and his woman Roselyn had their three kids, Javier, Xavier, and Evelyn, when they were both 18 years old. The two oldest Valdez cousins taught their children everything that their fathers taught them. Danny, however, had yet to have children. He was the playboy, and smashed women in every state he went to.

Tomas and Ricardo watched their kids take to the game like baby ducks on water. It came natural to the five of them, and with the teachings they had, they had sharper instincts, better character judgment, business, and hustler skills. They had no fear in their hearts, and they rode for each other without hesitation when one of them developed beef. They didn't care if one of them were in the wrong; family should always be there for family, no matter what.

Tragedy then again hit the family again when Tomás was found murdered in a graveyard in Pittsburgh, leaving behind his two young sons. His body was discovered up the street from where he grew up in out in the Homewood area.

It was found out to be a snake in Tomás's circle that had double-crossed him, when Tomás had gone to do a money pick-up. Not many understood why he went himself to make pick-ups, but his cousins did. They were taught by their fathers, that real gangsters handle their own business. Period.

After learning that the snake had gone to the Feds to seek protection for himself and his family, in exchange for divulging information on the Valdez family's business, Diego used his oldest brother's resources to find out what safe house the man and his family were being held by the feds at. The minute he found out, he pressed the green button and deployed his 100-man army to go get him. The deal had been for only the snake and his wife to be taken out.

Ricardo and his wife had been the ones who arrived first, with a mob of goons ready to light the place up. The plan was set, and a few of the agents guarding the house pretended to step away to go get food, while the Valdez clan handled their business. But two agents hadn't gone with and had no clue what was to be done. They opened fire on the Valdez mob, killing three of the Rastas. Ricardo and Roselyn were furious. They murdered the two agents, then after gaining entry to the house, they found the man and his wife, holed up in the attic with their children.

Being that they were soldiers, not monsters, the children lived; their parents did not. They were chopped up into pieces of meat by a machete, despite pleas of mercy, promising to leave the country forever.

Once word got out of the federal agents' murders, the federal eyes that had guided the Valdez family called fell back from them. Diego was furious with his son and daughter-in-law, but he understood. The top Fed demanded that Ricardo and his wife be turned over to him for prosecution. Diego refused. He had no choice but send his son and his wife away, to a country that had no extradition treaty with the U.S.

Danny, the only one left, took his cousins' children under his wing, as did the old heads whenever they came to the states, and raised them, teaching them not only the ways of the world, but to be knowledgeable of their Afro-Latino existence. Along with Danny, was his right hand that was more loyal and had more balls than most hardened gangsters.

A few years later, trouble struck again, when Danny got caught up with a truckload of cocaine. On a run back from New York, Illinois State troopers got on his bumper, up in the Gurnee area of Lake County. He took them on a high-speed chase that ended with spike-strips taking out his tire, and his truck flipping over. Everything had gone black when he wrecked his rig. When he came to, he was in an ER, handcuffed to a bed, facing drug-trafficking and firearm possession charges. Luckily, he wasn't being tried in federal court.

During the time he was in the Lake County Jail, the Valdez family's lawyers broke down the charges, and were so close to getting him off, when suddenly, Danny called it all off and accepted a plea deal for 25 years in prison, brought in secret by the state's attorney on his case.

The family was tripped out by the news. It fucked everyone's head up. His mother now had just lost both men in her life and had gone into a deep depression. Danny's right hand was broken to have lost her best friend.

Preparing to go serve his time, being the boss, Danny began electing people to hold certain positions in his family's businesses. For the top spot to run it all, he chose ChaCha. His confidence in her was not just because he'd taught her everything she knew, and saw how loyal and dedicated she was, more so because she already had boss qualities in her.

ChaCha was upset about her homie willingly going to prison and refusing to tell anyone why he didn't even fight, but she didn't continue to press. She knew one thing for sure... somebody had gotten to him.

One day, she would find who, and what made him take such a long prison sentence. And when she did find out, whoever had taken her homeboy from her, she was going to go from JLo, to Griselda Blanco... real quick.

While he was away, ChaCha ran the show. In the process, she kept the youngsters prospering and getting money, while doing her best to keep them from catching bodies. As they all got older, they followed in the family's footsteps and became drug-trafficking truck drivers, with companies of their own. With all that the family had lost due to the game, Danny and ChaCha hadn't exactly wanted that for them, but if the young ones just had to be a part of it, they made sure they had what they needed to succeed.

***

At such a young age, Javi had become a *very* successful man. He built his own multi-million-dollar business off of hard work and sheer dedication. Of course, being fortunate enough to be born into a notorious drug-trafficking family helped, but how he was raised, nobody gave him shit; he had to get his ass up and go get it.

Javi put his dirty clothes in a Gucci duffel bag and pulled out his iPhone. It was approaching 10:00 at night. He sent texts to his brother and sister, making sure they ready to ride. The monthly trip to the east, to pick up tons of the family's *white* gold from Jersey was upon them.

Responses from Xavier and Evelyn came minutes later.

Xavier: I'm ready bro

Evelyn: Duh nigga! Stop asking stupid questions, cabron!

Javi shook his head. His baby sister could be so snappy. Before Javi tucked his iPhone away, he sent attempted to call his cousin Macho again. Though incarcerated, Macho had a cell phone, as did Javi's big cousin Danny. Being rich in prison, one could get anything they wanted.

Javi got no answer. It was the tenth time in the last three days that he'd tried to call his cousin. He was really starting to worry.

Tucking his phone into his pocket, Javi lifted his head and smelled the mouthwatering aroma of Angela's cooking. He immediately got up with his bag and floated out of the room, towards the kitchen.

Goooooooddaaamn! She is so fuckin' thick! That's that Taino and African mix in her……..shit……….that ass is FAT! Javi thought to himself, as he watched the voluptuous Boricua finishing up his breakfast, while still ass-naked with her pumps on.

She'd made him *chicharrones de pollo* y *arroz*.

Sensing him, Angela looked to her left and saw the handsome Dominican there, gazing at her. She instantly started blushing.

"Ay, Jabier. ¿Por qué me miras asi?" she asked with a giggle.

He started walking towards her. "You don't want me to look at you?"

Her breath caught in her lungs as he stopped an inch away from her. He made her feel so shy, yet adored, and aroused, without even trying.

"Yah, papi. I lobe it when you eyes on me. I feel so 'sethy," she told him, her English so broken that he couldn't help but chuckle at her.

"Is that right?" he asked, wrapping his arm around her waist and pulling her to him.

Nervously and shy as hell, she nodded her head.

"It smells good in here. You did yo' thang, ma," he told her.

"Siempre por ti, papi. Ahora let me feed mi guapo tiguere."

Javi devoured the fried marinated chicken and rice savoring the deliciousness of it all. Ready to go, he gave Angela a quick peck on the lips and grabbed his bag.

"Te voy a extrañar, papi," she told him, hating that he was leaving.

"Oh yeah? You gon' miss big papi?" he asked, giving her the million-dollar smile that made her swoon over him.

Bashfully, she nodded her head. "I no wan' you to go, pero yo se you have to work. Just, por favor, cuidate."

"I'm always careful, lil' mama. I'm a muhfuckin' tiguere. It's the *ops* that need to be careful when they think about fuckin' with me and my family."

Angela giggled at him. It turned her on when Javi talked that gangster shit, because she knew it wasn't just talk. She knew the green-eyed *jabao* was really about that life.

"Ay, Jabier. You so 'sethy, papi. I 'lobe you."

Javi kissed her on the forehead and turned to head towards the front door.

Angela followed. As he was about to open it, she called to him again, halting him.

"Jabier?"

When he turned back to her, she grabbed his crotch, looking up into his eyes.

"Asegurate te llamarme cuando regreses por que voy a mamarte ese bicho *bien* rico, y te voy a chicharte hasta que no puedas mover las piernas."

She wanted him to call her when he got back because she was going to suck his dick *soo* good, then fuck him until he couldn't move his legs.

Javi chuckled at the freaky Puerto Rican. "I got chu', ma. Me voy," he told her, then headed out to her driveway and made his way to where his brand new *English White* Rolls-Royce Wraith sat on painted-to-match 24" Forgiatos.

29

Chapter 3
JAVI

Stop blowing that nigga's shit up, man! the king of the Valdez family had said.

Dammit. How the fuck he find out so fast? Javi wondered. He responded back. *Yo, cuz, his bitchass started it!*

Javi put the Rolls in drive and started rolling down Angela's driveway.

Danny's reply came as he reached the street.

Fuck that nigga, lil' cuz, but you got to remember, you a boss! Dude is a peon! Spilling blood doesn't make money. It makes shit hot1 You know that pussy muhfucka has cops in his family. Chill out. Be the boss we all taught you to be. Leave dude's bitch ass to JH.

Javi grinned to himself. JH was what Danny called ChaCha, his craziest goon, and his right hand. She was from *Jackson Height*, of Queens, New York. When shit hit the fan, not only did enemies have to worry about the Valdez family's Caribbean army, but they had to worry about the *colomborriqueña*. She was a true monster.

Javi paused at the tip of the driveway and typed a reply.

Aight, cuzzo. I'll fall back, but you know he finna try me again. He thirsty for clout. I can't keep allowing him to get his roll of and just let it happen. If I don't handle dude, you know Michelle will.

Danny replied back quickly.

I know. I spoke with her, too. Y'all chill out and let dude fuck himself. ChaCha already has plans in motion that he wouldn't ever be able to see coming.

Javi wondered what those plans consisted of, but didn't question it any further. He exited Angela's subdivision. He made his way to get on Grand Avenue, heading east to get to Highway Route 41, trying to clear his mind of Victor Gomez, and the constant attempts the Mexican cartel leader had recently started making back to back on him, and his drivers. He had to focus. The trip he was about to make was not one many others would ever be lucky enough, or brave enough, to make.

Javi turned on the music to get his mind right. King Louie's "*WINNIN'*" started playing, bumping from the stock audio system. He turned the music up and cruised, thinking about the business moves he had been wanting to make happen. He had plenty money, enough to do whatever he wanted. He also had plans to build his woman up and put her on a throne of her own. Her skill set consisted of more than just being a trained killer. She dabbled in designing fine jewelry, and what rich people didn't want some shine on their wrists, around their neck, in their ears, and on their fingers? It was time to extend his portfolio and make quadruple his money. He wanted to be a billionaire like his grandfather *soooo* damn bad, and had no plans on resting, even after it happened.

***

XAVIER

"*Nooo*, don't leave, bae!" whined Nena, a gorgeous yellow bone with the body of a goddess. "Your body feels so good next to me!"

She was a *baaad* ass chick. Her flawless high-yellow skin tone, her long dark and lovely hair, and her luscious curves were the reason Xavier was able to stand how crazy the Chicago-born belle could get.

Nena was from down Pilsen. She was 24-years old, mixed with Black, Mexican, and Greek. All three of her ethnicities showed. She was a firecracker when her fuse was lit; she was an exotic y, and completely crazy. The 5'6" beauty was often said to resemble the actress Lauren London, from the hit movie, '*ATL*'. She currently worked for Xavier and his brother's baby sister. It was always amazing for Xavier to see the sexy and sassy Pilsen girl at work. Not many women that looked like her did what she did.

Xavier, a 6'3" playboy, had a rich cocoa-complexion, with a fresh bald-fade haircut, and a lowly trimmed beard. He had the build of a WWF wrestler, but the fighting skills of a Golden Glove boxer. The 23-year-old was what many called a silent beast. He was a man of few words. His aura spoke for him.

With his GQ-model looks, his toned muscular body, tattooed on both arms and his chest, nearly every woman that encountered him swooned over him. Talk, dark, and handsome, with a bald-fade hair cut that had the *curls-for-the-girls* up top; Nena was gone over him. He was a humble Afro-Latino boss, with long money and swag.

"I gotta make moves, lil' mama," he said, in a deep velvety smooth voice that made her pussy wet again. "I don't make money by bein' in yo' bed."

"But you make me cum when you are. Isn't that better?" she asked, sitting up.

"No."

Nena scoffed. "Asshole."

He busted out laughing. "I'm just playin', shorty."

"Can I have some dick before you go?" Nena asked, standing up and stepping close to him.

"No."

Nena punched him in his chest. "OW! Dammit!" she cried, when her hand pulsated in pain from hitting his rock-hard chest.

Xavier laughed again. "Haven't you learned that punching brick walls isn't a good thing to do?"

"Shut up, nigga! I want some more dick before you go!"

"No."

"Why? Yo' ass finna be gone for days, man!" she complained.

"Because I gots to get showered and head out. Business always comes first, and you know that. Chill out. I'm only goin' to Jersey. I'll be back in a couple of days," he told her, then grabbing some clean clothes out of her closet that he kept there for times he stayed with her, Xavier headed to go get showered.

Nena laid there for a second. Then her mind started up again.

"Fuck that shit, joe. I'm finna drain that nigga before leaves up outta here," she told herself, then jumped up to go get at him in the shower.

***

EVELYN

"Mmmmm... hahahaaaa! Sssssss... oooooo, Eve! Shit! ¡Ay, mami! You fucking nasty bitch!"

Naked, bent over the dresser in the two lesbian lover's bedroom, in their big house out in the Gurnee area, Gloria moaned and giggled from the feeling of tongue in her ass. It had her toes going crazy in the sexy furry open-toe stiletto pumps she had on.

On her knees behind her milk-chocolate toned dominicana girlfriend, Evelyn's face was buried in between Gloria's fat 46-inch ass, licking and slurping her booty hole like it was made of Laffy Taffy. She ran her tongue around

33

the rim of it, and stuck it inside, swirling it around. Gloria squealed like a pig, then seconds later, she exploded so hard that her juices squirted out of her, soaking Evelyn's shirt.

Evelyn licked her woman clean, then delivered a hard smack to Gloria's ass as she stood up.

"Happy now?" she asked, her voice like that of a femininely tough hood chick.

Gloria stood up right and turned to face her girlfriend of four years. "No. I wanna' ride with you, bae."

"Sucks for you, biatch. This a family thing."

"I *am* family, Eve!"

"Just 'cause you're my bitch don't make you family."

Gloria mushed Evelyn's face. "¡Jodete, *cabrona!*"

"Nigga *fuck you*! Don't be mad at the truth, hoe," Evelyn shot back.

Both Dominican beauties stood five-feet-seven inches tall and had the curviest bodies. Gloria was dark and wore her auburn-dyed hair in a spirally afro, embracing her Afro-Latino heritage. Evelyn was golden-brown, like her oldest brother, and had long silky ass-length hair that she'd dyed a rich golden-blonde. They were both twenty-one years old and had known each other since they were in the 6th grade. Gloria had been born and raised down in Miami, until her parents moved her up to Illinois, raising her in Waukegan.

She met Evelyn, her brothers, and one of Evelyn's older cousins, when the Valdez posse got into a huge fight in the hallway at school. Knowing they were Dominicans, and her being Dominican, Gloria had always been raised to roll with her people. So, she jumped in and went at two chicks that were trying to jump the Valdez princess, while her big brothers and cousin were trashing some dudes that thought double-teaming each of them would be easy.

Gloria had seen Evelyn many times before. She'd been attracted to women since she was a kid. Having wanted to talk to Evelyn, but not knowing how to get at her, or if she even liked girls herself, when the brawl popped off, Gloria seized the opportunity… and it got her in with the beautiful golden girl, and her stupid rich family.

Dressed in a tight dark-blue long-sleeved shirt with *Balenciaga* spelled in pink letters across her bosom, tight black leather Balenciaga leggings, with pink Timberlands on her feet, and her luscious mane of golden locks, braided into two cornrows to the back, Evelyn was looked more like a hood chick with money, instead of the millionaire boss bitch that she was.

When she popped out she got swagged out, but typically, she rocked jeans, Mikes, Nikes, Tims, or sweats. She was a lesbian, but she was still very feminine. She was tough and fearless, as her mother had taught her to be, but was also a business-smart individual, as taught to her by her father, and her big brothers.

"You're an asshole, Eve."

"So? What's your point?"

"That you're an asshole."

"Good to know. Now I gots to go," Evelyn said, and kissed her girlfriend's lips and gave her juicy ass a slap. "Make sure you keep Nena's wild-ass in check while I'm gone, Glory-Hole," she said, calling her girl by the personal nickname she'd been calling her for years.

"Yes, *Booti-Full*," replied Gloria, calling Evelyn by her own personal nickname for her.

"Are you taking the Notorious P.I.G with you?"

"No. The job needs my full attention," Evelyn told her, just as her little 3-month-old brown furred pot-bellied piglet trotted into their bedroom. Evelyn scooped the little oinker up into her arms and cooed adoringly to him.

"Hiii, my cute little piggy wiggy! Mommy loves you! Yes, I do!"

The baby pig squealed and snorted happily, nosing Evelyn's face with his snout.

Gloria smiled at the picture-perfect moment.

"Aight, I'm out." Evelyn sat her piglet back on his hooves and grabbed her Leather Prada book bag.

"I love you, baby. Please, be careful," Gloria told her.

"I'm always careful, biatch. I love you, too," Evelyn replied, then headed out of her and Gloria's luxurious four-bedroom home, ready to go make a few more million dollars.

***

STACKS

"Nigga, yo' ass cappin', lord," Rambo said, finding it hard to believe what Stacks had just revealed.

In the kitchen of a small home, owned by the 30-year-old Mexican chick standing next to her younger 19-year-old brother, Stacks and his crew were assembled, sipping on Hennessy and rotating blunts of Purple Haze. When he told Rambo, Magali, and Mikey, they all had money signs in their eyes.

Rambo was a couple inches taller than Stacks, with brown-sugar skin, long dreads, and a more muscular frame. He was two years younger than Stacks. From the same hood as Stacks, Rambo was as 'bout it as Stacks was.

Magali, had an Aztec-brown skin tone, long black hair, standing a petite 5'3". Next to her was her long-haired brother Mikey. The young one was more fair-skinned, with big eyes, and had a peach-fuzz mustache. He stood the same height as his sister and was skinny from all the cocaine he did.

Stacks looked at his guy and twisted his lip up. "Fuck I need to cap, for, nigga? Bullshittin' ain't finna get us no money."

"My uncle works for the Rojas-Gomez cartel," Magali chimed in, racking her brain. "If it's the house that I *think* you're talking about, then my uncle runs that one."

Stacks looked at her with sudden interest in his eyes. "Yeah?"

She nodded her head. "I *told* you I got cartel in my family, bae," she said, walking up to him and wrapping her arms around him, looking up into his eyes. "I just didn't know the streets had the low-down on his spot. It'd be easy to get in there and stain his ass."

Rambo curled his lip up in disgust. He despised his guy's little bitch with a passion. To him, she was a snake. He just couldn't prove it.

"Why would you double-cross yo' own uncle, shortie?" Rambo asked suspiciously, as Stacks leaned down and kissed Magali on the lips.

A quick glance at her little brother, who looked down at the floor, then Magali looked at Rambo and answered his question with *major* attitude.

"I have my reasons, and don't call me no fuckin' shortie, nigga! Get it right!"

Rambo's hatred for her was shared by Magali. She hated *his* guts as well. They both wanted Stacks' attention. Rambo wanted it because he and his homie had grown up in the trenches together and were like brothers. Magali wanted it because she was in love with him and wanted him all to herself.

Rambo snapped. "Bitch, I'll slap the shit out cho' ass, joe!"

"Nigga you ain't gonna do *shit*, pendejo!" she snapped back, glaring at him with eyes full of fury. "I'm from south side, bitch! *Little Village*! Ain't no bitch in *my* blood! Fuck you talkin' about, joe!"

The two grilled each other, refusing to blink until the other did.

Stacks shook his head. He'd grown tired of his bitch and his guy arguing about dumb shit.

"Lord, chill out with all that otha' shit, joe," Stacks said, intervening before the two ended up going toe-to-toe.

37

Mikey stood there, looking at Rambo.

Rambo felt his eyes on him and looked at him.

"Fuck you lookin' at, lil' nigga?"

Mikey shook his head, staying silent.

"What about them truck-drivin' niggas I heard about?" Stacks asked Magali, bringing them back to business talk.

"Them niggas, honestly, Stacks, they some killers for real, joe. A *lot* of people been tryin' to get them up out the way for *years*, and they *all* failed. Even the *police* be tryin' but can't nobody get 'em. They the very definition of *plugged thugs*, joe," she told him. "Once a month, the Town and all around be flooded with that fire-ass yayo. It be coming from them, but nobody actually knows when they dip to get it, or how, other than in semi-trucks 'n shit."

Stacks started smirking then. "You still fuck with yo' uncle?" he asked her, switching topics as he felt that they should go after what would be a little easier.

Magali shrugged. "It's been a while, but I still have his number."

"Call him and tell him you tryna swing by at some point. Tell him you in school and yo brother workin', but y'all miss him and tryna come drink and smoke with him."

Nodding her head as she understood what he was thinking, Magali grabbed her phone off the table and made the call, putting it on speaker so everyone could hear. Stacks grinned as he listened to the girl put the game to the guy on the phone. By the way he was talking when she told him that she and her brother wanted to come over and get fucked up, Stacks knew that the guy was holding big weight. He started seeing dollar signs all over the place.

As Magali spoke to her and Mikey's uncle, Rambo shook his head. She was just too good at deceiving people for him.

If the bitch can pull it on her own blood, then she'll pull it even faster on muhfuckas that ain't related to her... her and her lil' weird-ass brother, he thought to himself, glancing at Mikey again.

38

"Aight, tio. See you then."

"Yup," the guy said, then the call ended,

Magali looked at Stacks with a cheesy-ass grin. "We in there like swim wear, papi."

Stacks nodded. "Period. After this, we on it with them truckin' muthafuckas, joe. Everybody else, too," he stated, pulling out his phone to make a call.

"Aye, lord?" Rambo called to him, halting him from dialing the number on his screen. "I got this Mexican nigga that got that shit, too, joe. Coke and dope, and he one of the guys. He a King, but from up Milwaukee; me and him been talkin' and he might be willin' to plug us."

"Them Kings from up Milwaukee are... *different*," Magali chimed in.

"Nobody asked you, *shortie!*" Rambo snapped.

"Bruh." Stacks cut in before they started bickering again. "*Fuck* them Milwaukee niggas, fam. They snaked out up there, thinkin' they better than Chicago. Hell naw!" Stacks refused, then he made his call.

Rambo held off on arguing. At some point, he would get Stacks to reconsider. He looked at Magali again. She looked back at him. They stared each other down while Mikey pulled a baggie of cocaine out and sniffed a bump off his long pinky nail.

Stacks waited for an answer that went to voicemail. Pissed, he called back-to-back five times, finally getting an answer.

"What the *fuck* do you want?" snapped the mother of Stacks' daughter, after he called her back-to-back eight times.

Stacks looked at the phone like *it* had lost its rabid-ass mind. "Bitch! Who the fuck is you talkin' to like that , joe?" Stacks yelled back.

"*You,* you bitch-made clown!!" Kenzie shot back. "Fuck is you blowin' me up for? I don't fuck with you! Leave me alone, bitch!"

"Kenzie, I swear on-"

"Lemme' guess! *On Ghost, On Ghost*! I don't give a fuck about none of that! It's 2015, stupid! Stop gangbangin' and get a fuckin job, you bum ass, dick headed lame!"

Stacks started grinding his teeth. He was beyond livid. He was ready to ride straight Kenzie's house and put her face through a wall.

"You cool, lord?" Rambo asked, seeing Stacks' eye twitching.

"Fam. I finna beat that bitch *sooo* muthafuckin' bad when I catch her. On Ghost I'ma beat the shit outta her ass, joe! Lemme see yo' keys real quick."

"Hell naw, nigga, you is *not* finna go over there now on that hot shit, lord," Rambo said, shaking his head. "We got bigger shit to be thinkin' about, not a bitch that can't keep clean panties."

"On *Ghost* I'm not. I gotta go buss' another move," Stacks told him.

Rambo then nodded and fished the keys to his SRT-8 Dodge Magnum from his pocket, tossing them to his boy.

"Where you going, bae? I'm tryna ride with you," Magali said, stepping in front of him.

"Naw, shortie. I'm finna go hit this lick real quick. I'll be back later," he told her, then made his way to the front door, stepping out into the darkness of night.

"Aw *heeeell* naw. Stacks!" she called after him, leaving her brother and Rambo in her kitchen, running to catch up her boo.

Outside, he was walking up to Rambo's blood-red Magnum, which sat up on 24" Choppers, painted to match the whip.

She called to him again, catching up to him as he was opening the driver's door.

"You really just gon' bounce on me, though, nigga?" she asked, damn near pushing him up against the door.

"Shortie, what chu' on? Yo' ass doin' too much right now," Stacks told her.

Magali grabbed at his crotch. "Oh yeah?" she asked, dipping her hand down into his True Religion sweats, wrapping her hand around his cock, and slowly jerking on it. "Am I doing too much *now*?"

Stacks couldn't help but smile at her. "You gon' play with it, or buss' down and put this dick in yo' mouth?"

Magali smirked seductively, then she dropped his pants and boxers to his ankles, freeing his thick 9" pipe. Without any hesitation, she dropped down and started pleasuring him. She deep throated all of him without a problem, using one hand to cup his balls and massage them, while she stroked his shaft with the other.

Stacks groaned in bliss as his little freaky Mexican belle domed him up. He grabbed her head and started fucking her face until he felt his nuts tightening up. A minute later, he came in her mouth, filling it up with hot gooey sperm. Magali swallowed it all with a smile, looking up at him with stars in her eyes.

"Did you like that, baby?" she asked him, still with his dick in her hand.

"Definitely did. Now take yo' freaky ass back inside and have that pussy wet for me when I get back," he told her, pulling his clothes back up.

"Why can't I come with you, Stacks?" she asked, getting up off her knees.

"Bitch! Stop fuckin' questionin' me and do what the fuck I said!" he snapped.

"Okay! Geez, you ain't gotta yell, nigga, damn!"

Stacks hopped in the car and started up the powerful Hemi engine. He backed out of her driveway, and headed off, disappearing from her line of sight seconds later. Magali cursed under her breath, then turned, only to damn near run right into Rambo.

She jumped back, startled by his presence. "Fuck is you sneaking up on me for, you fucking weirdo?!"

Rambo smirked at her. "My bad," he said sarcastically, then stepping around her, he headed towards the street, just as a dark-colored SUV pulled up.

Magali watched him hop in, then it pulled off. "*On* my momma, he gots to go. After this move, Stacks is gonna be *mines*!" she declared, before heading back into the house.

Mikey was snorting lines of coke when she walked in. "Want some?" he asked her, holding up a straw.

She went to join him and snorted up two big lines. "Stop staring at Rambo like that before he starts suspecting about you. You know him and Stacks both *hate* jotos."

"Fuck them. I am who I am. When are we takin' them out, though?" he asked.

"When I fucking say so, Mikey! Don't be fucking questioning me, okay? I got this!"

Mikey watched his sister snort a couple more lines, then march off towards her bedroom, slamming the door shut.

"Bitch," he muttered under his breath, then lowered his face down to the table to do some more lines.

Chapter 4
JAVI

Arriving in Wadsworth, Illinois, a small town just west of Zion, right on the border of Illinois and Wisconsin, Javi made his way to his self-made trucking company, of which he called *Dedicated Transport, LLC*. He'd built it with one truck, hard work, and money he'd stacked up driving a truck for his father, hauling *anything* that got him top dollar, including *tons* of cocaine.

Altogether, he owned 32 semi-trucks, with a few spare trailers and trucks in case of break downs and lengthy maintenance. Trucking had been the biggest thing in his family, since his grandfather, and his great uncles started importing tons of cocaine into the country, back in the hippie days. It was a no brainer that he, his brother, and sister, along with their cousins, all became truck drivers, *drug-trafficking* truck drivers at that.

On the legit side, Javi's company was made up of three divisions. He headed the *Dry-van and Intermodal* freight transport part, along with a crew of nine, all from the streets. His younger brother Xavier ran the *Heavy Haul* and *Specialized Freight* division, and the *Auto-Transport* division was run by Javi and Xavier's younger sister Evelyn's.

Everyone employed there was dedicated to getting money. They were all loyal, and straight from the streets. Javi, his brother, and their sister treated everyone like family instead of just drivers. Their father had always taught them to treat people that worked for them, or with them, as their equals, instead of their subordinates.

On the property was a big 85,000-square-foot service and repair garage. With six long and wide service bays, an office, and everything a truck company owner would need in his or her garage, Javi's expensive fleet of trucks and trailers barely ever stopped working and making top dollar.

Out to the side of the garage, another structure with five wash ports for keeping trucks and trailers clean and shiny. Javi didn't have to ever tell his drivers to keep their rides clean. They already had pride in their rides, especially since their rigs were what made them big bucks every week. Not a single one of them made less than six figures per year, and that was without all the bonuses that Javi constantly gifted them all with.

Javi owned *more* than $15 million dollars' worth of equipment alone, not counting the worth of his land *and* the building. The amount of money he made per *month* was enough to make Lebron James jealous, but it didn't come easy. It took *big* money to make even *bigger* money.

Pointing a separate key fob at Bay #1 of the garage, Javi hit the button to open the bay door and disarm the building's alarm. As the door started rising, the motion sensor lights inside came on. They shined down on the brand-new custom-built Kenworth W900L, sitting inside the long parking bay.

Javi parked his Wraith at the office entrance door and hopped out, walking to the open bay door. He stood in front of the elegant-looking rig and smiled at it. He was a true truck-nut that loved customized big rigs.

Javi bought the expensive rig with zero miles on it and immediately took it out to Jersey to a truck chrome shop and customizing businesses owned by his cousin Tool. Dropping close to $200,000 on the $225,000 W900L, the truck was turned into a rolling piece of art that turned the heads of people that normally paid no attention to big rigs.

It was painted cocaine white, and had so many chrome and stainless-steel exterior parts that made it flick so hard that it turned the heads of people who normally wouldn't pay a big rig any mind.

Its custom chrome grille, bumper, headlights, and the custom V-shaped windshield drop-visor that hung down low from the top of the cab and made the truck look pissed off, while the big, tall chromed 8" monster exhaust stacks made the truck look like it had devil horns.

The frame had been stretched, giving it a *hotrod*-look, and custom suspension let it sit low to the ground while it rolled on big shiny 24-and-a-half-inch wheels. All the chrome and stainless-steel exterior accessories paid big compliments to the paint job. The biggest portion of Javi's money came from trafficking the white, so it only made sense to push a white truck that was the Rolls-Royce of big rigs.

While the outside turned heads, inside was just as eye-catching. Behind the cab was a spacious mid-roof style sleeper berth that Javi had did up to rival the comforts of a Rolls-Royce Phantom. Whenever he had to take a break from driving, or on long hauls and had to sleep on the road, he relaxed and slept in true luxury.

Smiling at the aggressive-looking front of his W9, Javi took a second to appreciate what drug money bought. Even on the legit side of his world, Javi found himself wishing that more men and women from urban communities got into trucking. If more people realized how much money a truck driver made, trafficking illegal goods or not, there'd be a *lot* more people of color on the road, and taking over the always-thought-to-be-white industry. But, being the owner of said truck, the possibilities of financial freedom were endless.

Javi entered the bay and went to the driver's side of his W9. He opened the door and climbed up inside the customized interior, done up with white Rolls-Royce leather seats, glossy wood floors, a wood grain dash, fitted with chromed gauge bezels and switches, a custom wood and chrome 4-spoke *GT Classic* style steering wheel, with the shifter to the eighteen-speed transmission matching.

The Apple iPad sitting on the dash was used as an Electronic Logging Device. By law, truckers hauling interstate commerce across stateliness were required to keep logs, detailing their trips, and keeping records of the hours they drove, made stops, took breaks, and took time completely off from driving. Javi used a driver-trip-log app to stay in compliance with the *Department of Transportation* and the *Federal Motor Carrier Safety Administration's* rules and laws. Out of all the illegal goods that Javi hauled, he *had* to take the job serious.

He logged into the app and selected the *On-Duty/Not-Driving: Pre-trip* status. Before each trip, during, and after, safety inspections were mandatory. Driving an unsafe truck was just stupid. Million-dollar lawsuits were filed against truckers and truck company owners because of truck crashes and often won. Javi wanted to continue *making* millions, not lose them.

Sitting in the driver's seat, Javi glanced down the garage to where a nearly new glossy red Peterbilt 388, built into a 10-car transporter sat, with a blown engine. Two months ago, he paid close to three hundred thousand for it, and there it was, sitting, with a destroyed engine, not making any money. It was driven by Nena, one of Evelyn's drivers. Javi knew it was completely driver-error that the engine was blown. She was irresponsible when it came to keeping up on routine maintenance. Javi could easily get another motor put in. He had a few spares in the tool room, but he felt Nena needed to understand how bad she messed up by not thoroughly keeping her truck inspected. It paid her bills, so why wouldn't she take care of it like *she* bought it?

Deciding she needed to learn a lesson, Javi had it put in the garage and refused to let her behind the wheel of one of his spare rigs.

Getting back out of his truck, Javi went and unlatched the W9's engine hood on both sides, then tilted it forward, exposing the clean red and chromed-out ISX Cummins, a powerful beast of an engine that Javi had upgraded with high-performance diesel parts from *Big Boss*, resulting in 725 horsepower. The motor alone was worth just over $30k.

"Hello, you sexy red beast, you!', Javi said to the monster engine, then got to checking everything inside the motor bay.

***

"¡Si, patron! I see that pinche dominicano right now! He's in the garage checking over his troca!" said Solo, whispering into the Bluetooth earpiece in his ear, as he laid ducked down between two of the Dedicated Transport semis, parked in the company's yard. He was ready to put in work for his boss on Javier Valdez. "I can get him right now, patron! Just say the word and the pinche puto is dead!"

"No!" Solo heard the boss say. "I sent you there for one reason! To get inside his garage when he leaves! I want you to plant the listening devices in his office and around the service area! ¡Nada mas, *cabron*!"

Solo cursed. "But, boss, I can-"

His words were suddenly cut off when he was grabbed from behind. Solo yelped in fear as he was lifted off the ground. When he was turned around in mid-air, Solo nearly shit his pants when he looked down into the eyes of the *biggest* man he had ever seen in his life.

"*Ta'u I lou pule ua e toilao I le misiona, ma o le a e oti I le po nei, vale,*" the gigantic Samoan bone crusher declared in his native language, glaring up at Solo, with fire in his eyes.

***

XAVIER

Lil' Durk's *Dis Ain't What U Want* pounded from three 12" JL Audio subwoofers in the back of Xavier's glossy Santorini Black Range Rover HSE Supercharged, rolling on 24" Forgiatos. Behind him was his baby sister, whipping her new silver metallic BMW 7-series Alpina B7, which rolled on chrome 22"Forgiatos.

As he came upon the Dedicated Transport yard, Xavier saw through the chain-link fence, Javi's *humongous* 6'9", 400-pound driver, Tank, dragging a man that was kicking and screaming, across the yard from where his big Freightliner Classic XL was parked by a few other rigs. Xavier hit the gas as he turned inside, sister following suit, then floored it up to where the big man and Javi were, skidding to a stop and hopping out to lend a hand.

***

JAVI

Javi ground his teeth in anger as he watched Tank bring forth the intruder.

"¡Sueltame!" the Mexican shouted, trying to fight to get loose. "Get the fuck off me!"

Tank was a brown-skinned man, with long hair, tribal tattoos on his arms, chest, and legs. His massive 6'9" frame was terrifying. He tipped the scales at just over 400 pounds. Getting out of his grasp was *not* going to happen.

When he'd gotten the guy to Javi, he let him go.

"¡*Chingate, puto!*" the spy shouted, attempting to hide his fear.

In a desperate attempt to make it out of there with his life, he reached down to grab the .380 Walther PPK, strapped to his ankle, concealed under his jeans.

Tank quickly grabbed his hand and twisted it so hard that the Solo's wrist bone snapped.

"Aaaaggghhh!", he screamed, grabbing at the protruding bone.

Tank reached for Solo's ankle, felt the gun, and took it.
CRACK!

He smacked the living shit out of the spy with his pistol.

"Shut the fuck up, pussy!" Tank roared, ready to attack him again. "Don't cry now, bitch! Accept that you fucked up like a man!"

Chuckling, Javi shook his head. "Who you workin' for, my man?" he asked, in such an eerily calm way that Solo was even more afraid.

Solo looked up at the green-eyed man he'd heard so many things about. Glancing at the Samoan, the dark-skinned guy, and the beautiful light-skinned girl that had pulled up and hopped out of the Beamer like she was the jump-out cops, he gathered his bravery and responded as if he wasn't shitting bricks.

"Fuck you! You're all gonna die!"!"
SMACK!

"Shut up, bitch!" Tank yelled, smacking Solo again with his pistol.

"¡Que se joda! Tank! Bring that bitchass nigga inside the garage! I'ma make him scream *louder* than Mariah Carey!" Evelyn declared, then in a flash, she took off into the garage, heading for the tool and parts room.

Tank chuckled and looked at Javi. Javi nodded his head. Solo tried to get up and run, but Javi clipped his legs from under him and made him face-plant into the ground. The giant then grabbed Solo, snatched him up off the ground and carried him in, kicking and screaming like a child en route to an angry mother, with a leather belt.

"You good, bro?" Xavier asked him.

"No. That bitchass nigga coulda' had me, bro," Javi admitted. "Now we gotta add a security entrance fence. Come on and let's go watch sis make this bitch scream."

***

EVELYN

"Aaagghh! Aaaagggghhhh!" he screamed, as the hot flame of the acetylene torch fried the skin between his ass crack.

With his pants and boxers yanked down, Tank held the spy down on the ground, making sure he couldn't get up as Evelyn flamed his asshole up.

"Yeah, bitch, scream!" she mocked, watching the skin bubble and bleed. "¡Te jodistes con la familia error cabrón! ¡Por eso te vas a sufrir!

Tank chuckled at her. Spanish wasn't his natural language, but having been employed by Javi for so long, he'd learned a lot. He knew that she had just told the guy that he fucked with the wrong family, and for that, he was going to suffer.

Javi and Xavier stood watching, half excited, half horrified.

"Damn… sis is crazy, bro," Xavier said.

"This is definitely a new one for the books," Javi agreed.

"Okkaaayyy! Okay! God okay! I'll talk!!" the Mexican screamed.

Evelyn pulled the torch back. "Speak on it, bitch! Who the fuck sent you over here?!"

The man started crying when he saw the murderous look in her eyes. He was so scared that he was suddenly rendered speechless.

"Aye, aye, aye. Shut that cryin' shit up, bitch," Xavier told him. "Don't nobody wanna' hear that shit."

Javi shook his head. "You know what… cook his ass, sis," he told Evelyn, not needing the man to say who sent him.

He already knew.

"Nooo! Nooo! Noooo!!" the spy screamed when Tank got up and yanked the man up off the ground, holding him for Evelyn.

She put the fire to his throat and burned right through it. The flame severed his head in less than a minute. It fell to the ground and rolled, while his body remained held up by Tank.

"Damn… did I do that?" Evelyn asked, looking down at the dead head.

The guys busted out laughing.

"You most definitely did, shorty," Tank said. "Don't trip; I'll get rid of this bitch."

Javi told him to hold up, then he went into the dead man's pocket. Pulled out the phone, that had call time that was *still* going. "I wonder who's on the line," he said, going into the settings and unpairing the Bluetooth earpiece and putting the phone on speaker.

"I'm guessin' the person on the line isn't a phone sex operator," Javi spoke, then waited for a reply.

Tank and Xavier snickered while Evelyn was still breathing heavily, fuming that an enemy had just tried them *again*.

They all heard a chuckle come from the phone. "No. But I *am* going to fuck *you*, you punk bitch mother fucker."

"Well, that's pretty damn gay of you to say, dontcha' think? How about you bring yo' bitchass here yourself, instead of sending mules to die. You and I can have a nice *long* talk."

"How about I erase your whole pinche familia off the fucking planet, puto? You wanna' blow up my shit like you think you're a gangster, eh?! I can show you a real gangster!" the man replied, with a venomous tone.

Xavier chuckled. "Well now that we know you're that lame-ass paisa that runs Fast *Lame* Logistics, are you done makin' empty threats?"

"Haahaa! Empty you say?"

"Yeah, bitch! Empty!" Evelyn jabbed. "Come on! Talk that gangsta shit! ¡No seas un *miedoso*, bitchass nigga!" Evelyn cut in, telling him *'Don't be a pussy'* in Spanish.

"I know you are, but what am I?" the man laughed. "I'll tell you this, though, Señor Javier Valdez. I swear on my *abuela's* life, you, your pinche brother and sister, *todos ustedes cabrones están chingada!*"

"Ya *mama's* fucked, bitch," Javi replied. "Escuchame bien, puta. Fuck *you*, *fuck* yo' *lame-ass* cartel, fuck yo *bitchass* daddy, and *fuck* yo grandmamma, too! *No* Vaseline! Come see me when you think you ready, hoe! Now I gots to go get this money. Buh-bye now, mamahuevo."

Javi ended the call then. Evelyn busted out laughing at him.

"Eeeeee, my big brother is a muhfuckin' *G!*" she said. "Now if he could *stop* cheating on his lady, then we would be all good!"

He looked at her with furrowed eyebrows. "So, it's *you* that's been tellin' her that I be creepin' around?!"

"No se que tu hablas," she said, looking away from him.

"Yes, you do know what the fuck I'm talkin' about! Stop snitchin', *Eve!*"

"Then stop fucking cheating on her! ¡*Charlatan!*

"Aye!" snapped Xavier, stepping in to stop his quarreling siblings. "Don't we need to be getting' on our way?"

Tank stifled a laugh. Javi and Evelyn were hilarious when they argued.

Javi groaned. "Yeah, you right. Y'all go get y'alls trucks checked and we gon' hit it. We got money to make."

"*We got money to make*," Evelyn mimicked, walking away to exit the garage to park her Beemer and pre-trip her truck.

Javi shook his head. Xavier snickered then left out himself to park his Range and inspect his truck as well.

"Don't trip, bruh man," Tank said to Javi. "I'll clean this up. There's a pig farm up the road; I bet they like barbacoa."

Javi laughed, dapped Tank up, then went to start up his Kenworth.

Chapter 5
VICTOR

Sitting in the driver's seat of his new yellow Lamborghini Aventador Roadster, Victor Gomez was seeing red. The 33-year-old chicano was livid that his spy had been caught up. He knew for a fact that the overzealous clown would never be found. He was beyond tired of how every attempt he made to get at the young Dominican, he lost. Now, he was ready to get back into the field *himself.*

Victor was a fair-skinned man that looked more like a high school star athlete than the leader of a vicious Mexican cartel that his father had built, back in the 70's. He kept his hair on the top of his head a little longer, parted on the left and slicked with gel, while the sides and back closely faded. He kept a clean shaven face and mostly wore custom-tailored suits. The mocha-colored Salvatore Ferragamo suit he had on fit his 5'10" frame perfectly. On his wrist he had on a customized Richard Mille, and around his neck, he wore a simple gold chain.

Victor grew up in the cartel world. He was born in Guadalajara, raised by his father mostly, who had been a well-respected man. Having been taught everything by the seasoned cartel veteran, Victor was groomed for the job that he now had as the boss, and he had no intentions on being anything less than the greatest. Javier Valdez and his family were preventing that.

To Victor, being the leader of the Rojas-Gomez cartel was a great honor. He had an army of a few hundred men and women, all with either military training or street smarts. When he was a teenager, he was sent to live in San Antonio. His father wanted to see how Victor did, running a small crew of his own, before putting him in a seat of real power. Victor excelled, taking over Texas with ease, and increased the wealth and clientele of the organization.

His next task was migrating to the Midwest to northern Illinois. Victor immediately jumped in and started making a name for himself amongst all the street mobs and other underworld organizations operating in the ILL-State. He started a trucking company to bring up product from Mexico and distribute it to his customers.

He soon found out that he wasn't the only one that had developed self-shipping methods. When he learned of how the Valdez family's strong grip on the logistics industry, he grew extremely envious of them. Though he could admit that they were like a well-oiled machine, he wanted them gone. The Midwest was to be his, and *only* his. But sending goons at the Valdez youngsters proved to be far from enough to get them out of his way. They were truly innovative with their methods of murder, and they *all* had high body counts.

***

He arrived at his company's biggest terminal, up in Milwaukee, just before midnight. It was a massive property that housed 200 trucks and 250 trailers. It was his main branch location. His office was there, attached to a dispatch center, with a big service and repair garage. Daily, it brought in over $300,000 per day.

Entering the security gate when the ex-Mexican Special Forces operative manning the gate house opened the gate up, Victor rolled into the property and headed towards where his office was.

Brooding on how he could possibly get Javi and his siblings gone, Victor thought about all the failed attempts he'd made in the past year. He'd sent gangbangers at Javi, dirty cops, other cartels, and even a few Middle Eastern extremist organizations. The ones that agreed to get at the young Dominican, once Victor put a very high price on Javi's head, they *all* failed....*horribly*. The others had ties to the Valdez family and ended up coming at Victor for him trying to send them on a suicide mission.

The beef with Javi was now personal, since the young gunner had the audacity to run up in one of his truck yards, kill all his security guards, and destroy every truck and trailer there. To him, he didn't care that *he* himself had started it, nor that there had been peace between his family and the Valdezes for so long. Victor wanted the Midwest for himself, and he was going to take it. Anyone who tried to stop him, he was going to have them and their families murdered.

Fuck peace! And fuck the Valdez family! I'm gonna' kill 'em all! ¡Pinche putos! he thought to himself, as a line of red Fast Lane trucks pulled off from the loading docks, heading towards the yard's exit lane.

He rolled past them and came to where his office's entrance door was. Parking and killing the big V12 engine in the rear of his exotic car, Victor got out and made his way inside.

At the desks in the dispatching center, a group of beautiful women were working, staying in communication with the Fast Lane drivers that were out there on the road. When the boss walked in, they all swooned over him, hoping one day to replace the 38-year-old brown-skinned chicana that awaited him by his office door.

Victor saw Esperanza there, dressed in a red ribbed short sleeved turtleneck top, with a tight mid-thigh length plaid Burberry skirt, and red stilettos on her feet. Her long dark-brown hair was styled like she was going to enter a beauty pageant. Her lips shined with the glossy red lipstick she had on. Big gold hoop earrings dangled from her ears, black eye shadow gave her the *smokey* eye effect, and around her neck was a gold necklace.

"Is everything okay, Señor Gomez?" she asked, as Victor put his eye to the retina scan pad at the side of his office's door.

"No!" he snapped, as the door unlocked. "That *fucking* Dominican destroyed millions of dollars' worth of my shit at my damn yard!" He pushed the door open and entered the plush Presidential-style office. "I swear on my grandmother's life, I'm gonna *kill* that kid!"

Esperanza followed her boss into the office and closed the door behind her, locking it. She watched as he marched around the custom Mahogany wood desk and plopped down into the leather high-backed chair. He sucked in a deep breath of air, then shouted out at the tops of his lungs, before slamming his hand down on the desk.

"Señor Gomez, calmate," she told him, making her way over to him. She walked around his desk and came to a stop right in front of him. "You cannot let a kid get you this upset. You are a grown-ass man. Personally, I think you should stop trying to compete with him. Your father negotiated peace with the Valdez brothers a long time ago, and things were good until you started fucking with that boy."

Victor looked up at her and was suddenly filled with rage. He shot up from the chair and grabbed her by the throat, startling her. She shrieked and tried to pry his hand from around her throat, but he was too strong for her.

"¡*Perra*!" he hissed through clenched teeth. "I didn't fucking hire you to run your mouth! Let me remind you what you are here for when you are not in your pinche cubicle!"

Victor forced her to turn around then he slammed her face down onto his desk top. As he used all his muscle to hold her down, Esperanza begged and pleaded with him. Her pleas fell upon deaf ears as he pushed her skirt up over her ass, exposing her tiny thong.

"Mr. Gomez wait! I'm sorry!" she cried as her thong was snatched out of her ass crack. "Please! I was just trying to help!"

Victor ignored her as he dropped his pants, freeing his throbbing cock. He smacked her ass cheek hard, then he rammed himself into her dry butt hole. Esperanza tried to scream but his hand covered her mouth. He maliciously violated her until he busted his nut inside of her anal tract. When he pulled out of her, yanked her up and smacked the hell out of her. Esperanza yelped and fell to the floor.

"Let that be a lesson to you, *perra!* Don't you *ever* again tell me what to do! *I* run this! *Me!* Now get the fuck up and out of my office before I have my men chop you up into pieces and stuffed into a barrel of acid!"

Crying from the throbbing pain in her ass, Esperanza dragged herself up off the floor and limped towards the door, cupping her sore ass.

"Pull your skirt down, whore!" he yelled.

She obeyed before she opened the door and left out, whimpering and sniffling.

Victor grabbed the phone receiver on his desk and hit a button. A second later, a deep voice came out of the intercom.

"Yeah, boss?"

"Esperanza is coming out of my office. Go get her and get rid of her. Make sure she is never found. ¿Comprendes?"

"Copy that, boss. I'm on it," the man said, then his voice was gone.

Victor then pulled out the top drawer to his desk and got out the little burner phone stashed away in it. He powered it on and called one of the three numbers stored in it.

"¿Si, patron?" answered Gordo.

"Are you on them?" Victor asked.

"Affirmative, sir. We're on their tails right now."

Victor nodded his head. "I swear, Gordo, if you fuck this up, you and your men, will die, but not before I have your wives and kids killed in front of your eyes. Get the fucking job done!"

There was silence that lasted ten seconds. Gordo then replied, "Yes, sir. Copy that," then ended the call. Setting the phone down on his desk, Victor inhaled a deep breath then exhaled. He tried to calm himself, but he was livid.

Why is it so hard to kill a 24-year-old kid? he wondered to himself, then out loud, "Pussy motherfucker. Let's see you and your *pinche* brother and sister escape a trained Mexican death squad, bitch."

He chuckled at himself, then reaching back into the desk drawer, he grabbed a manila envelope that was filled with cash. He tucked the burner phone back in, grabbed the key to his Lambo, then headed out to go pull up on one of his associates, to get the individual on board with him, against the Valdez family.

***

STACKS

Half past eleven at night, Stacks crept through the back yard of a moderate sized house, with a Glock in his hand. He had a red bandana tied around the bottom half of his face, and his hoodie pulled up on his head. The backyard was dark, giving Stacks the perfect cover to creep right on up to the back of the little house.

A window to the left of the concrete steps, leading to the back door, was lit up. It was open. Stacks could hear what sounded like running water, dishes clanging, along with music playing. He glanced around at the two houses on the sides of the targeted home; no lights were on. It was a Friday, so he was sure the neighbors were out getting lit.

Smirking, Stacks stepped up onto the landing of the stairs. He twisted the doorknob and discovered that the door was unlocked. Gently pushing the door open, he stepped into a brightly lit hallway, then quietly closed the door behind him.

He could hear Lil' Durk and Dej Loaf's hit song, *My Beyonce* as he stepped towards where a doorway was to his left, with steps leading to the basement ahead of him.

Advancing a few feet forward, Stacks peeked around the corner of the doorway. His eyes went as wide as dinner plates, when he saw a ridiculously thick chick in the kitchen, washing the dishes.

She was dark like Godiva chocolate and had long dreads with red tips that fell to her ample ass. She looked to be about five-seven, or eight.

With only a set of red lace thigh-high stockings, held up by a red garter belt around her waist, shiny red latex calf-high stiletto booties on her feet, Stacks' dick started throbbing in his True Religion sweats.

Goooooodaaamn! On Vicelord, that bitch is thick as fuck, joe! he thought to himself, as his eyes traveled down to her horse-sized ass, which had a big red five-point star tattooed on the right cheek.

Shaking his head, Stacks clutched his gun tighter in his hand and crept up behind the girl. When he got to within a few inches of her, he put the barrel to the back of her head. The second she felt it, she froze.

"Turn the water off, and if you scream, yo' brains will be all over the window in front of you. Nod yo' head if you understand, bitch!" Stacks growled through clenched teeth.

The woman nodded her head, then she turned the water off.

"Good. Now turn the fuck around so I can see yo' face."

He took a step back and watched as she slowly turned to him. The second he saw the soft features of her beautiful face, Stacks felt like he'd just hit a lick.

This bitch is so damn bad! Stacks again thought to himself, awestruck by her beauty.

The girl stood a few inches shorter than him. Her 36DD breasts were so plump and succulent, like cantaloupes, and had Hershey's Kisses for nipples. Out of all the tattoos she had, Stacks noticed the one above her right titty that said *D & J 4ever* tattooed. Her 28" waist matched her wide hips that flowed down to thick thighs. Behind her, she had that OH-MY-GOD-size 50" ass. Her lips, full and juicy, kissable and worthy of being sucked on.

Stacks looked down into her soulful brown eyes for a second and almost got lost in them. He blinked, bringing himself back so he could get on with his mission

"You always do the dishes naked like that?" he asked her, as he stepped close and ran a trail along her jaw line with his Glock.

The song changed to Ginuwine's *Role Play.*

"Only when I'm expectin' my baby daddy to come beat this juicy-ass pussy up," she told him, in the sexiest hood chick-type voice.

"Oh yeah? That nigga on the way here right now?" He grinned at her then.

"Yup. He is."

"Hmmm." Stacks lowered his cannon down to her chest, and traced circles around her right nipple with the barrel. "You think he gon' be mad if he come up in here and find me fuckin' his thick-ass bitch?"

The girl smirked at him. "Would you really give a fuck?" she asked.

Stacks snorted. "Nope."

"You break up in my muthafuckin' house to talk?" she asked, giving him a defiant look now. "Or you got somethin' on yo' mind? A bitch got shit to do, joe. And like I said, my baby daddy is on his way."

"Bitch! *Fuck* yo' baby daddy!"

"Naw *don't* fuck my baby daddy, *nigga!*" she snapped back. "Fuck his *bitch!*"

"Say less, bitch. Drop down and put this muthafuckin' dick in yo mouth and suck on it real good! 'Til I buss' a nut all down yo throat!"

Stacks set his cannon on the counter next to the sink as she dropped down to her knees. She yanked his sweats and boxers down to his ankles. Eye level with his throbbing 10-inch cock, she smiled at it.

"Now *this* what a bitch needs right here," she said, kissing the tip of it. "Some *real* dick."

"Bitch, what the fuck I say?! Put it in yo' mouth and suck on it!"

Stacks grabbed his dick with his right hand, her head with his left. As she opened her mouth, he put it down her throat.

She girl closed her mouth around it and let him start fucking her face. His balls slapped her chin repeatedly. She felt the tip touching that dangling thing in the back of her throat. She gagged, but didn't resist. Stacks grunted and cursed. Her mouth was so warm and wet. It felt like a tight pussy.

She sucked his dick like a porn star on molly and coke. She took it out of her mouth and spit on it, then she took it back in and went crazy, sucking and jerking him fast. Stacks felt like his knees were going to give out.

"Shit! Goddamn, bitch! I finna buss' already!" he told her, feeling his nuts tightening up.

She took over then as she tasted pre-cum. Grabbing his thick length with both hands, the girl twist stroked as she sucked. Stacks groaned gutturally as she brought him even closer. But he didn't want to bust his nut just yet. He wanted to see if she had that bomb between her legs.

"Fuck this shit, shorty!" he cursed, snatching his dick out of her mouth. He yanked her up from off her knees and grabbed her by the throat. "I need some of this pussy, bitch! Turn around and grab the counter!"

She did as she was told. Stacks slapped her ass hard. She shrieked, but looking back at him with the sexiest fuck-face, he knew she liked it.

"Tell me you want me to fuck you, bitch!" he demanded of her, then smacked her ass again.

"Shit! Fuck me! I want that dick up inside me!"

SLAP!

"Louder bitch! Scream that shit!"

"I want you to fuck me! Fuck me hard and crazy, goddamnit!" she shouted, then she bent over, tooted it up, and looked back at him.

Stacks gripped his piece and put the tip to her soaking wet opening. He rubbed her swollen pussy lips, getting his dick wet.

"Stop fuckin' teasin' me and put it in!" the girl growled between clenched teeth.

Stacks smacked her right ass cheek. "Bitch! Shut the fuck up! *I* run this shit, joe! Fuck you talkin' 'bout!"

After a minute, Stacks slid up in her. He stretched her tight walls out as he inched his way further in. The girl moaned loudly, feeling him slide all the way up in her tunnel.

Stacks' eyes rolled to the back of his head. She felt so good around him. He started stroking her, gradually speeding up. Twista & The Speedknot Mobstaz' *Dreams* came on just then as Stacks began hitting the pussy so hard and fast that the girl could barely catch her breath.

"Shit! Oh God, yes! Fuck me! Just like that!" she cried out, as he jack-hammered her.

After almost ten minutes, Stacks felt her contracting around him. She was so wet, leaking like a broken faucet. She screamed out that she was about to cum. He went even faster. Seconds later, she exploded so hard that she almost passed out from it.

Stacks felt his nut coming on strong. He announced he was about to bust. The girl hurried to pull him out of her. She pushed him back to the fridge and dropped back down to her knees. She took his dick back into her mouth and sucked until he came to within seconds of exploding.

Taking his cock back out of her mouth, she jerked his shaft and made his cum all over her face, catching as many hot globby droplets as she could with her mouth open and tongue out.

"Shiiiittttt!" Stacks nearly screeched as she milked him for it all. "Goddamnit! Whoooo!"

She emptied him all over her face, then as his dick began going soft, the looked up at him. Seeing his contorted face, she busted out laughing.

"Eeeeeee, joe! Bae, I be havin' yo ass lookin' like yo' just ate some Sour Patch pussy!"

Stacks busted out laughing at her. "Bae, yo ass wild as hell," he told the mother of his one-year-old son. "What the hell made you come up with this role-playin' type shit anyways?"

He took her hand and pulled her up from her knees then pulled his boxers and sweats up.

"I watch a lot of porno, Dontae. Duh! Yo ass be watchin' it, too, so don't get to cappin' 'n shit, nigga."

"Yo ass wild hunnid, joe. On Ghost."

Jasmine smiled at him. "I'm the same as you, bae. We from the same damn block in K-Town and came up with the same people."

"Hell yeah, we did, baby. I love that you and I made it through all these years and still goin' strong."

SLAP!

"Aye!" Stacks jumped away when his son's mother out of nowhere slapped *thee* shit out of him. "Fuck you do that fa?"

Jasmine started laughing her ass off.

"Bitch, yo' ass high?!" Stacks looked at her like she was nuts.

"Naw, I ain't high yet, but I definitely got some fi'-ass green in my bedroom. I slapped yo' ass 'cause you fucked around on me with a white bitch."

Stacks rubbed his face, salty as hell that she'd just fired him up like that.

"Kenzie ain't even white; she Armenian and Cuban," he told her.

"I don't give a fuck! She ain't *Black*!

Stacks started laughing then. "You the only bitch I'll ever let slap me and not get they muhfuckin' jaw broke."

Jasmine stepped up close to him, with cum still on her face. "Is that right, Dontae? You be beatin' up other bitches?"

"Yup! *Fuck* all these bitches!"

She grabbed the collar of his shirt then, and kissed him, not giving a damn about if he wanted her face on his.

She pulled back after nearly a minute of lip boxing with her baby daddy. "I got somethin' I need you to come beat up... again," she purred, looking at him with pools of liquid desire.

"Eeeeee, joe! On Ghost, I'm ready!" Stacks told her. "Where my son at, though?"

"At my momma crib. We can go get him tomorrow. I been waitin' on yo ass all day. You finna come handle yo business right the fuck now, and you ain't gon' be done 'til I got fo' of 'em. You dig what I'm sayin'?"

"Oh yeah! Let's go!" Stacks said, then surprised her by scooping her up into his arms and running her to her bedroom to give her what she wanted, just as Young Jeezy's *Tear It Up* featuring Slick Pulla came on.

Chapter 6
JAVI

Leading the way in his flashy Large Car, Javi nodded his head to "Lil' Wayne's *Pussy, Money, Weed,* while pushing his truck at just over 80 miles an hour, riding it like it was a STR-8 Challenger, he aimed to make it to Indiana within an hour of leaving the yard. Behind him was Xavier in his own decked-out Electric-Blue W900L, of which he had two of. Evelyn, in her custom, emerald green, metallic 2015 Volvo 780, brought up the rear, keeping up with her big brothers

The trio pushed hard down the E-Way, blazing a trail through Chicago. They passed through the Chicago Skyway Toll Booth's *I-Pass* lanes, and a short time later, exited out of Illinois and entered Indiana.

As Javi merged onto the East-West Toll Road, the music stopped, and a call came in the made Javi smile his ass off.

"Eeeeee, mamitaaaa! ¡Que paso, bonita!" Javi pressed the answer button on the Pioneer's screen, answering the call via Bluetooth.

From the speakers around the cab and in the speaker came Michelle's sweet giggling.

"¡*Diablos*, papi! You sound so sexy!"

Javi chuckled. "Yo' ass crazy, baby. What up, though? Why you still up?"

"I can't sleep. I miss you. Plus, your voice gives me confidence before I got to work."

"Confidence? ¿En serio?"

"Yes, papi. Seriously. When I think of you, I'm motivated to do my job right, so that I can make it home to you."

Javi couldn't help but smile at that.

"Are you smiling right now?" Michelle asked him.

"How you know that?" he asked back.

"I can hear it."

Javi busted out laughing. "You never cease to amaze me, love."

As they talked, Javi's mind took a trip down memory lane, back to when he first met his woman. He, his brother and sister, along with their older cousins, had all gone to New York, out to Washington Heights of Manhattan. The big Dominican area was home to many of their family members. Back in 2010, five years prior, they'd all been invited to where a big summertime block party was jumping off. Javi and his siblings loved the Heights. The strong Afro-Latino culture, food, etc; any chance they'd gotten, they went to the east coast, be it New York, or Pittsburgh.

As he hung with his family, Javi had spotted her. She was looking unbelievably good in a skin-tight denim dress, with denim high-heeled boots on her feet. Her hair had been a rich gold color and hung freely under the denim New York fitted she had on. Javi swore he was looking at a Dominican Christina Milian.

Javi's slightly older cousin Macho, whom Javi was so tight with, that they were often thought as brothers instead of cousins, saw that Javi was stuck on the sexy brown beauty. He told him, 'Man up and go get at lil' mama before someone else does and we gotta go jack 'em up'. Javi got on it and went to go get at her.

Michelle was with a few of her girls and a cousin, when she spotted the thuggishly handsome green-eyed man with Iverson braids coming towards her. She immediately felt her breath catch in her lungs. He was one of the most handsome men she had ever seen, and as he came towards her, she found herself feeling like she had a competition subwoofer, beating in her chest.

Javi got to her, and not actually having a clue what to say or do, he made the most brazen move: he took her hand, then pulling her to him, he kissed her... long and hard.

Michelle wasn't the least bit creeped out by it. The pussy got so wet by his brazenness. Her friends all went wild about it. When he pulled back, Javi felt empowered. He *then* introduced himself. Once the introductions had been made he offered to get her a drink and they distanced themselves from the party.

That day their vibe was something that could never be replicated and they became attached at the hip. They dated for a few months, before Javi got her to agree to move to Illinois with him. He was very happy to see that when she discovered how rich he was, that it really didn't seem to affect how she was towards him. She was still into *him*, not what he could do for her. But as they grew closer, and Michelle learned of exactly who Javi's family was, Javi found out about Michelle being a contract killer.

She told him exactly how she got such a profession. In a nutshell, a guy in her neighborhood was known to be a creep. One dark stormy night, Michelle went to one of her friend's houses to smoke a blunt and drink with her, only to discover the door to her apartment was ajar. Stepping in, Michelle found that the place was trashed. Panicking, she raced towards her friend's bedroom and saw her homegirl laying naked on the floor, bleeding from her nose, mouth, and ears. She'd been raped and beaten to death.

The cops stepped in, but nothing happened. Nobody was arrested. People in the community were outraged, but nobody did shit. Her friend's father was a well-known drug dealer in the area and had long money. He put a $25,000 bounty on the guy's head, which got a lot of people looking for him.

One day, while Michelle was on the bus, coming home from school, she spotted the dude walking down the street. He was wearing a disguise, but she knew for a fact that it was him.

She immediately got off the bus and followed him for blocks, until she saw him enter a seafood restaurant. She strolled past and got a glimpse of him through the window. It was crowded, but she was able to see his face clearer. She went to the end of the block, then doubled back, forming a plan in her head. Taking her hair out of the ponytail it was in; she fluffed it around so that most of her face was hidden. When she got back to the restaurant, she entered and was seated.

Seeing him sitting at a table near the kitchen, Michelle noticed how on edge the creep looked. Guilt filled his eyes and he was likely terrified. It was without a doubt that he had heard about the price tag on his head. People in New York killed for mere fist fights. $25,000 was enough to make someone blow his brains out in *front* of cops.

A minute later, after Michelle placed her order, she saw the guy get up and head towards the bathrooms. She went into her book bag and got out a pair of scissors, then tucked them into the waistline of her skirt. She took a deep breath, then got up from her table, walking past tables filled with people, not making eye contact with anyone.

She was *geeked* to see that the door wasn't locked. She wasn't sure if it was a bathroom built to accommodate more than one person or not, but the time was now. She had him trapped, and was *not* letting him leave alive.

Slipping inside, Michelle *did* lock the door behind her. There were two stalls to her left, and two urinals to the rear. Looking under one of the stall doors, she saw his crummy boots, then she heard snorting.

Knowing he was in there getting high, Michelle pulled her scissors out and got ready. She went and stood right in front of the stall door and waited.

The toilet flushed, then the door opened. With white powdery residue in his nostrils, the guy looked at Michelle.

"Well, hello, cutie. Came to give big papa some of that sweet young pussy?" he had asked her, revealing cracked yellow teeth when he smile.

Michelle clenched her teeth and flew into a raging frenzy. She charged at him, jumping up and tackling him to the ground. He fell back and hit his head on the toilet. Michelle stabbed him in his face, repeatedly until it was barely recognizable.

She managed to pull herself out of her blacked-out state and got off the dead pervert. Covered in his blood, she quickly went to the sink and washed her hands, then she pulled his clothes off and put his shirt and pants on to cover her own bloody clothes. She dropped the bloody scissors in the toilet and flushed multiple times until she was sure they were gone, then hurried to leave out of the bathroom.

As incognito as she could be, Michelle made it out of the bathroom, grabbed her book bag and got up out of the restaurant. When she made it to the bus stop, just as the bus was pulling up, she hopped on and sighed in relief. It was over. She had avenged her friend.

Days later, as she sat on the stoop of her mother's brown stone, a dark-colored SUV pulled up in front, and two big Dominicans got out from the front. One walked up to her and told her that his boss wanted to talk to her. Michelle got up and followed him to the rear passenger side window of the SUV. The window rolled down, and she saw her friend's father inside.

"Get in, Michelle," he had told her, scooting over to the other side for her.

Michelle did as he told her to. The man handed her a brown paper bag with the $25K in it. Michelle's eyes went wide in shock, not because of the money, but because she hadn't told anyone that she killed the guy.

Her friend's father smiled, knowing she was baffled as to how he knew. He explained to her that the seafood restaurant was his, and his men had been tailing the guy all day when a few anonymous calls tipped them off. They saw her tailing him as well and told the boss. He instructed them to allow her to get at the guy, knowing how close she was to his daughter. They reported that only *she* came out of the bathroom, wearing the creep's clothes, then when they went in to find him, he laid dead with a bunch of bleeding holes in his face.

From that day one, Michelle had become a contract killer. Her friend's father employed her and sent her on high-dollar missions all over the country, and not once had Michelle failed a job.

Javi caught *his* first body when he and Michelle were at a bar, having a good time. A clown that couldn't control his liquor felt it was okay to follow her into the lady's room. Javi had just happened to be going to the rest room himself, when he heard screaming inside. Recognizing his lady's voice, he charged in and found the man forcing Michelle into the stall, to do God knows what. Javi beat the man to a bloody pulp, then drowned him in pissy toilet water.

***

"Am I supposed to stop being amazing?" Michelle asked her man, bringing him back from his trip down memory lane.

"Hell naw. But you're amazing without even tryin' to be, amor."

"Aww! My nigga is so *sweeeeet*! Te lo juro por Dios que cuando yo regrese te voy a dar demasiao toto y tal vez te canse de chingarme."

Javi busted out laughing at her. "Michelle, I could *never* get tired of fucking you," he told her. "And I can't wait for you to get back home either," Javi told her. "Me voy a comerte esa chocha bien rico y despues voy a metetelo hasta que venga duro."

"Ay, nooo, Javi! Pineapples!" she whined, realizing that it wasn't a good idea for talking dirty when they were so far away from each other. "¡Tenemos que parar! We can't be saying things like this when I'm not there for you to do that shit to me," Michelle whined.

"Oh naw? So I can't tell you how good I'ma eat that pussy when you get home? Make you cum so hard that your legs go numb?"

"No!"

"What about… .slidin' this big fat platano inside that wet ass pussy? Beatin' that toto up until you cum like an exploding volcano?"

"*NO!*"

"Hmmm… can I tell you how good I'ma-"

"Nooo! Javier stooopp!"

He laughed so hard that tears filled his eyes.

"That's *not* funny, mamao. You're gonna make me punch you when I get back."

"Ain't nobody afraid of them little-ass hands you got, bae."

"Uh huh. These *little-ass* hands have special powers."

"Ohhh whoa whoa whoa. Diablos, mamita. You just went ham on me, yo."

Now Michelle laughed. "Right. Shut cha' ass up and quit tryna' heat me up while I'm all the way in oil field country, asshole."

"Mmmm… asshole… wait 'til you get back… I'ma put my face all up in that big ol' juicy booty."

Michelle stayed silent for about ten seconds or so. Javi laughed his ass off at her again, knowing she was likely in her hotel room, wet as hell, yearning for him.

"Your ass is grass when I get back, yo, si sigues hablando esa 'mielda.," she said, after a few more seconds of silence.

"And your ass is getting' pregnant when you get back," Javi countered." I'ma make yo' ass the Dominican Octomom."

"Bet. Eight babies by the man I love? It don't get no better than that," she told him. "Unless you wanna give me *ten* babies."

"¡Coño! *Ten*?! Ten lil' ones runnin' 'round with nappy afros and pigtails?"

They both busted out laughing at the visual.

"I'm dead-ass serious. Ya' ass is gon' be workin' out with me, when we do that shit. I gots to keep this toto nice and tight for you after every baby I pop out."

"Oohh yeah! That is definitely a good idea to me! I got a *reeaal* good work out for us!"

"Which'll likely lead to more babies, 'ya fucking freaky-ass Dominican dude. Better eat ya' Wheaties, then, nigga, 'cause you gon' have a lot of work to do," Michelle told him.

"Work! Work! Work! Work! Yeah I know I gots that work! I keep her pussy soakin' wet! Always goin up her skirt! Twerk! Twerk! Twerk! Twerk! Make that juicy booty twerk!" Javi suddenly rapped out loudly.

Michelle howled in laughter at him. "¡Ay, Dios mio, this nigga is cray-cray, yo!"

"You already know, mamita! Crazy for you!"

"Oh, my God, I fucking love you so much, papi!" Michelle cooed, still giggling. "Pero you should stick to driving trucks... *not* rapping."

"And I fucking love you, too, mi tigueras*a*, pero shut up," he replied.

Michelle burst out laughing again.

Chapter 7
JAVI

A little over six hours later, having made it through Indiana, Ohio, the trio was now on the PA Turnpike. They kept on turning and burning east until they got to Monroeville, then they got off the interstate at Mosside Boulevard, jumped onto Route 22, and headed east to Murrysville.

Their family's biggest truck yard terminal sat on the side of the road. It was the first location their great Uncle Pedro purchased when their cocaine empire was being built. The armed guards at the gate and in the security shack, were already expecting them and, had the gate open. Javi, Xavier, and Evelyn threw the deuces up at the ex- Green Berets and Marines as they rolled past them.

PJ&D Transport, LLC Murrysville's yard was like a small neighborhood. Forty acres of commercial land; built on it was a massive diesel repair/maintenance garage that was bigger than a football field, with a lot of service and repair bays, and a big dispatching center. The truck fueling station was combined with a regular gas station to make life for all the employees a little easier, with major discounted gas prices. There was also truck wash and car wash ports, and recently built, was a big luxurious 5-star luxury hotel, with 500 grand suites, free of charge to anyone working for any part of Valdez Industries, Inc.

At the creation of the company, Pedro, Juanito, and Diego, made a vow to treat every single one of the people they hired, as if they were family. They didn't care how many people that would end up being. Since they got into business, the three had kept their word, and so did their sons, and now *their* children were striving to do the same.

Men and women with extensive military training and other highly trained backgrounds were placed around the yard. There was a lot of very valuable merchandise there, and the ol' Valdez heads wanted nobody but the best and the most fearless to protect their investments.

Rolling past the gigantic employee lot that was the size of a Wal-Mart, they passed the huge truck parking area, littered with all sorts of semi tractors, dump trucks, and roll-off dumpster trucks. Many of the drivers that were in their rigs, preparing to take off, or having just returned, shouted out to Javi and his siblings on the CB radio; their trucks were very well-known on the road, and by Valdez family employees.

As they approached the area where the enormous diesel station was, Javi saw the customized X-edition Peterbilt 379 Extended Hood. The fancy rig was painted in Ferrari's *Rosso Corsa* Red paint. It was so shiny that looked like red chrome. The front wheel fenders *were* chrome. The long list of custom exterior accessories made the special edition semi look like it belonged in a truck show.

The driver of the half-million-dollar show-quality truck was like big cuz *and* big sis to Javi, his siblings and his older cousins. She was also like godmother.

Turning to pull up to a pump, Javi heard her voice come from out of the CB.

"¡Oye, mira quien estan aqui! ¡Los tiguerasos de Wauk-Town!"

Javi chuckled to himself as he grabbed his CB mike to reply,

"You know it! The Dominicans are coming! 'Erybody *run!*"

Her laughter came afterwards.

Javi parked at a pump right next to where the X-edition sat. As he put on the brakes and put the shifter into neutral, he saw the owner sitting behind the wheel; in the passenger's seat, he saw her tiger-striped monster, looking at him, with his tongue hanging out.

"Aw shit... she dun' brought Pablo out. Somebody gon' die," he half joked, knowing that the brown brindle Presa Canario was a trained killer at just 12 months old, and was *very* protective of his owner.

Xavier and Evelyn parked their rigs at other pumps, amongst where a few other PJ&D Transport trucks were fueling up. The three put their logs onto *Off Duty status*, cut their engines off and got out.

The driver's door of the X-Edition opened, suicide style, as Javi approached. Evelyn ran past him, beating him to the driver as she stepped her Timberland-booted foot out onto the painted fuel tank. She was extremely excited to see big cuz was rolling with them. When Javi saw the look on ChaCha's face... the text from Danny suddenly hit him again.

"ChaChaa!" Evelyn shouted out, as the six-foot Amazon warrior-type beauty got out of her truck, throwing her arms around her and bear hugging her.

Ximena, whom everyone called ChaCha, was a gorgeous Puerto Rican and Colombian woman. She was a butter pecan-complexioned chick, in between petite and voluptuous, from New York's Jackson Heights, Queens area. Her long jet-black hair was in two long braids to the back, and on her head was a New York fitted. She had hypnotizing Arctic Blue eyes that were as frosty blue as the waters in a winter wonderland section of the world.

She rocked a black work shirt, with PJ&D Transport in red letters on the back, and a picture-perfect decal of her X-edition Peterbilt under them; tight black skinny leg leather pants accentuating her shapely thighs, legs, and ass; down on her feet, ChaCha sported a ridiculously expensive pair of *Red October* edition Air Yeezy 2s.

On her wrist she sported a new rose-gold Ferrari Hublot with a red dial. Hanging around her neck was a long yellow-gold Cuban link chain, fitted with a Puerto Rican flag pendant, embedded with red, white, and blue baby diamonds.

At just 30 years old, the colomborriqueña was a billionaire. All the work she'd been putting in for the family, since she was in her late teens, had put her in a seat of power, when the boss needed her the most. Every penny she had, she earned. She had a wealthy-woman swag, but what people respected about her, was how ChaCha could sit back and never physically work for the rest of her life, but was still the type to get up out of the office, and get behind the wheel of her truck, to go haul some loads, just because she was a truck driver at heart.

She was the Valdez family's very own Jennifer Lopez, a queen in their eyes. But when shit hit the fan, she went from Jennifer Lopez to Griselda Blanco......*real* quick.

***

CHACHA

"Javier, why you still blowing that bitchass nigga's shit up?" ChaCha asked. "You *and* Michelle?" she added, with an accusatory eyebrow.

He couldn't help but chuckle at the fact ChaCha knew everything, likely before Danny did.

"He started it," Javi told her, then explained to her about the spy that had invaded his turf, and how he had no choice but clap back. "And you *know* my lady ain't never been the type to not ride with her man."

ChaCha shook her head. "¡Hijo de la gran puta!" she said of Victor Gomez, infuriated that the guy just wouldn't stop.

She looked at Javi. "I want to be pissed off at you, but I understand. You just should've called me about the whole thing. We do have people that can handle little things like that, papacito."

"Fuck all that shit, ChaCha," Javi said. "His bitchass could've killed O-Boy! Fuck *all* his people!"

Xavier and Evelyn stood off to the side, not saying anything. They understood what their big brother was saying, but they also knew that ChaCha was the boss.

"We have the fucking Rasta's Javi! Jamaica's men are paid to handle shit like that!" ChaCha shouted angrily, taking a step towards Javi with her fists balled up.

Hearing his owner snap, ChaCha's massive *Dogo Canario* started barking out of the passenger's window.

"Cuz! I *can't* let his bitchass keep comin' at me! Come on, now, prima! I ain't built to call in someone else to handle *my* beef! *Fuck* all that shit, joe! I came out of my O.G. a muhfuckin' G, and I'ma go out like one!"

Evelyn and Xavier both took a step back. They had never seen their big brother get loud with ChaCha, nor had anyone else, that lived to tell about it.

Glaring at him, ChaCha grinded her teeth angrily. "See... the other day, I was talking to Diesel," she said, calling the family boss by the nickname she'd been calling him since the day she met him. "*And,* he told me that you and Michelle were out there shooting up the competition's trucks, blowing his shit up. I said *nooo,* that isn't how Javi is. That lil' nigga is a *business*man; that crazy shit is what *Macho* does. Then, I find out that you *are* doin' that crazy-ass shit!"

Javi kept his mouth shut. He had no bitch in his blood, but he knew for a fact that if he tried to debate with Jennifer Blanco... he'd get punched.

He relented, not wanting any smoke. "Sorry, cuz," he said instead of arguing further, looking down at the ground.

"You will be, if I hear you fucking with dude's bitchass again. Chill out, yo. I have someone working him; word on

78

my motha', son, that nigga on borrowed time. Lemme' do what I do best: handle business."

"Okay. But if your… person that's working him, is doin' they job, then how a spy get in my yard with a pistol?" Javi asked.

"What?" she asked, with a raised eyebrow.

Attempting to take some of the heat off her brother, Evelyn stepped in to explain to ChaCha what had happened at the yard.

ChaCha immediately went and got her phone from her truck. She came back to where the three stood and made a call. Despite it being just after midnight, the call was answered after three rings.

"Hello?" a woman answered, sounding groggy.

"*¡Puta!* ¡Te pagué por hacer un trabajo! ¡Lo juro por Dios, si lo jodes, te vas a sufrir *doloroso*! ¡¿Me entiendes?!" ChaCha snapped.

"Y-Y-Yes… I *am*, though, ChaCha! Why are you snapping on me?" the woman asked nervously.

"A spy sent by that *hijo de la gran puta* that you *work* for, made it into my baby cousin's yard, with a gun! If it wasn't for the dumb motherfucker choosing to lay under a truck that my cousin's driver had been sleeping in, he *might* not be here right now!"

"Oh, my God! I am so sorry! I swear! I'll put more bugs around his office! I'll follow him everywhere! I swear I won't fuck up again!"

"If you do, *bitch*, I'm feeding you to my dog!" ChaCha told her, then ended the call.

Javi shook his head. "What is it with you and Michelle feeding people to dogs?"

ChaCha laughed. "Free food, cabron. Now y'all fuel up so we can go and park. We need to rest up so when we get there, we're good enough to hook up and pull right out."

***

After they fueled their trucks up and got a bite to eat at the small café, Javi, Xavier, Evelyn, and ChaCha parked their trucks and went to get rooms in the yard's hotel and caught eight hours of shut eye. When they woke up, they all felt re-charged and ready to hit it.

They pre-tripped their tractors, then wasted no time heading off, making their way back on the PA Turnpike.

Javi led the way east. Xavier was behind him, Evelyn behind Xavier, and bringing up the rear was ChaCha. Javi only wondered how long that would last. He knew that ChaCha had an engine under the hood of her truck that could make a Bugatti seem like a Mustang.

A thought hit him as Mike Jones's *Cuddy Buddy* featuring Trey Songz, Lil' Wayne, and Twista pounded. He tapped the screen to the Pioneer and brought up ChaCha's name. He hit *call* and waited for her to answer.

"Yo?" came her voice from the speakers, after two rings.

"¿Prima? You heard from Macho lately?" Javi asked. "I been callin' cuzzo, textin' him; he ain't got back at me at all. He in the hole or something?"

He heard ChaCha sigh.

"Not sure, papcito. You do know what time of the year it is right?" she asked.

"Oh……damn……that is right." Javi cursed himself for forgetting that the current month they were in, was when Macho and his big brother Tool, had lost their mother to cancer, exactly one year ago. "Fuck, yo. I know Tonio and Tool feelin' fucked up right now."

"We all are, Javier. Word, yo, Cristina was the sweetest and most caring person that anyone could ever know. I really wish I could've gotten to know her a little better."

Javi nodded his head. "Well, do you know when he's getting' out? Last I heard, he was real close."

"Yes. He is. But he doesn't exactly want anyone to know, so don't ask me to betray his trust. You'll see him when he touches down. Okay?"

"Yeah. Aight, cuz," Javi said, then ended the call, and letting his music fill the cab again.

Cruising along, Javi got lost in his thoughts. He hoped his cousins were okay. He didn't know when he was going to see Macho, but he knew he was about to see Tool, as soon as they got to Jersey.

Chapter 8
EVELYN

"What do you want, Nena?" Evelyn answered her phone when she saw Nena was calling again, for the sixth time in a row.

"Uh… how come my truck is still sittin' in the garage?" she asked.

"Bitch! I *knooow* you ain't asking me that dumbass question?! The question is, how come you not taking better care of what pays your bills, pendeja?!"

Evelyn heard Nena smack her lips. "Maan, I didn't mean to fuck my truck up, Eve. Stop tweakin' on me. Lemme' use the Coronado so I can keep workin'."

"HA! No!"

"Eve! For real! I really need to keep making money! I… I got things that I'm really gonna need to be financially stable for, comin' up in….like….seven to eight months."

"I do *not* give a 'mudderfuck! You should've thought about that when ya' ass wasn't drivin' right, *Azalea*!" Evelyn shot back, calling Nena by her government name.

"*Eeeve*! Please, man! I swear! I won't fuck the Coronado up! And… I'll help fix my truck, too! Please?"

Evelyn groaned in frustration. Nena was her homegirl. She felt bad for her, to be honest. She knew the Pilsen girl was really alone in the world, and her job was literally her life. If it wasn't for Xavier, and her career, many people thought Nena would've committed suicide, from all the hardships she'd endured in her past.

"Aight, Nena. Dude, I swear on my big cousin Tommy, if you fuck that truck up, too, not only am *I* gonna put my foot up yo' ass, but you finna have to deal with Javi, and very likely, Michelle."

She heard nothing but silence for a minute, which told Evelyn that Nena had gotten the point.

"Okay. I'll be careful. I promise. Thank you, Eve," Nena finally said, sounding relieved.

"Uh huh. What's comin' up in seven to eight months?" Evelyn asked.

"Um… I'll tell you when you all get back," Nena told her, then ended the call.

Evelyn shook her head. "That bitch is weird as hell, man," she said to herself, then started rapping to Dej Loaf's "*ME, U & HENNESSY*" when she turned the music back up.

***

XAVIER

Lil' Wayne's *Grown Man* featuring Curren$y cut off as a call came through. Xavier pressed answer on the Kenwood's touch screen and answered the call coming from another one of his chicks.

"Yo?" he answered.

"Hey, sexy papi," purred Keisha, Xavier's chocolate-complexioned freak.

He chuckled. "Whaz' goodie, wifey lady?"

She started laughing at him. "Nigga, you *know* yo' ass ain't tryna make a bitch yo' wife."

"One day, maybe. What up, though? Why you up so late?"

83

"Because I'm horny, and I miss you and I can't sleep well without your body bein' next to mine after I buss' all over that dick. When do I get to see you again?"

"I'm on the road for a few days, then I got a real big load that I gotta pick up and take down to Texas. Might wanna grab a Snickers."

Keisha smacked her lips. "That's crazy. Don't you got people that work for you? Why you can't, like, make them do it and come hit this pussy? My fingers and my silver bullet ain't like the thang I really need, baby."

Xavier busted out laughing at her. "What is it that you need?"

"You, nigga! Stop actin' dumb. I need that dick *and* them lips, Xavier!"

"Oh. I must be doin' it right if you sound like you ready to box if I don't come break you off soon."

"Mmmmhm....you aight, and hell *yeah* we finna box if you don't hur'rup and get cho' ass back to me. I be wakin' up and my pussy be wet as fuck dreamin' about you."

"Eeeeee, listen to you! I be getting' the pussy wet and I don't even be there. I do believe that I *am* that nigga!"

Keisha laughed her ass off. "Uh huh. I'ma tell yo' ass this, though, *nigga*; when I see yo' lil' other bitch, on my *momma*, I'ma *dog-walk* that hoe, joe. Real talk."

"My other bitch?"

"Yeah, nigga! That lemon-head-ass bitch! You *know* who the fuck I'm talkin' about, Xavier!"

He did: Nena.

He chuckled then asked, "Why?"

"The bitch egged my car yesterday! This is the sixth time!"

Xavier howled out laughing.

"Nigga that shit ain't funny! I had just gotten it washed when she did that shit!"

"She's like a bird; a clean whip is a perfect target for her."

"Oh, so you cool with that ratchet-ass shit, huh?"

"No, but you *did* put shampoo in her gas tank, Keisha," Xavier reminded her, laughing at the memory of Nena pulling up into the yard in her $85,000 BMW, blowing bubbles out of the exhaust pipes, right before the engine completely seized up.

"Well, I ain't have no sugar." Keisha busted out laughing at herself. "Fuck that bitch and her car. What's she drivin' now anyways?"

"My Chevy, and if yo' ass do *anything* to it, I'ma fuck you up. Real shit."

He heard her smack her lips.

"Fine then. Be captain save-a-hoe, but when I catch her, I'ma baby-powder smack her ass the fuck up."

Xavier shook his head. Thinking of when he saw something like that on the movie *How High*, happening to Nena, he burst out laughing.

***

As the sun began rising into the sky, riding up Interstate 78, the quad left out of Pennsylvania, and entered New Jersey. The kept breezing along east until they got to Elizabeth, then got off the highway and headed for Tool's big oil and fuel refinery.

ChaCha led through the busy heavy industrial city to where *East Coast Fuels, Inc.* was. Two lines of *PJ&D Transport* semis pulling empty tanker trailers took up the two main entrance lanes to the massive 110-acre property.

ChaCha led the three into the furthest lane to the right, where an auxiliary lane was. The heavily armed guards, all ex-Special Forces and Marines, posted inside the booth, had the gate opened for them before they even saw the red Peterbilt coming. The guards posted up outside all nodded their heads and waved hello to the Valdez convoy.

The refinery was the way point for the tons of imported Valdez cocaine, fresh off the Valdez family's own cargo vessel. There, the coke was disguised in many different forms, allowing it to be transported in bulk, in top secret. Cops, state troopers, or county sheriffs, looking to try their luck at popping off a load of Valdez gold, would have to go through so many hurdles to do so, that they'd give up.

ChaCha headed towards the very back of the refinery, where a big building with an inside-loading dock was. Arriving there, she, along with Javi, Xavier, and Evelyn, saw ten bulky-looking black Hummer H2s on off-road wheels and their front ends fitted with rammer guards. They were parked in a line. The mob of Jamaican gangsters, protectors of not only the transporting convoys, but of the Valdez family, were posted up outside of the beefed-up SUVs.

The leader of the crew of Caribbean goons was a man that everyone called *Jamaica*. He was a six-foot tall dread, straight from Kingston. He was a light-skinned man, with long dreads, graying at his temples from being in his late 50s. He was the right-hand man of Diego Valdez, Javi and his siblings' grandfather. Jamaica had been through hell and back with the Valdez brothers. In no way shape or form did he have any plans on retiring anytime soon. He was a protector, through and through. Javi, Xavier, and Evelyn, in many ways, were like his grandchildren. He would lay his life down to make sure they were always safe when it came to handling business.

Jamaica was leaned up against the custom grille of a new shiny black tri-axle Kenworth W900L heavy-duty *'rotator'* wrecker. The big fancy tow truck belonged to the giant golden-brown skinned Dominerican standing next to him.

His long dreadlocks were freshly twisted at the roots. His beard/goatee along with his baby hair line was both lined up razor-sharp. He was a big bulky man with tatted-up Anaconda arms. His broad shoulders were wide, and his barrel chest poked out like a wrestler's.

Tool was *huge*! He intimidated people without even trying to. The twenty-eight-year-old was technically second in charge of the Valdez family, right after Danny Valdez. He had a major hand in the family's operations, but he was more of a background player. Tool ran his multi-million-dollar businesses on the daily basis, as his own priority, but when he needed to be, he was fast to hop on the front lines with his family, especially when big moves were to be made.

His refinery was his biggest money-maker; along with it, though, Tool owned a big towing and recovery business that had an auto and diesel maintenance and repair division with it; he owned a few auto scrap yards out in Pennsylvania, not far from his neighborhood. He had recently begun to establish a custom truck/trailer/bus building business, specializing in *glider-kit* trucks, which were custom-built rigs, special ordered by people to have their own everything in the builds. For anyone wealthy enough to afford the cheapest builds, at no less than $125,000, Tool and his crew of skilled diesel technicians would build their dream truck that they could feel like they're the shit in when they put it on the road.

As far as family business, Tool was next in line to reach billionaire-status. With the inheritance from his and his younger wild-card brother Macho's father passing away, he was more than halfway there. He had yet to touch the billion-dollars inheritance that he and his younger brother split 50/50. The millions of dollars he'd earned from trafficking tons of cocaine, was what he used to build his empire. His investments had paid off long ago.

***

Five trailers sat by themselves outside of the building. Two were 45'-foot long propane-transporting tankers that had a carrying capacity of 10,500 gallons of pressurized liquid gas. They both had red diamond-shaped hazmat placards with the numbers *1075* displayed on them, and under the four hazmat identification numbers, was

Flammable Class 2. The other three were 42'-foot long chemical transport tankers that could carry up to 6,200 gallons of liquid bulk. They had *black and white* diamond-shaped hazardous material placards on them, with *Corrosive Class 8*, displaying the hazmat numbers *1778*, displaying that the loads were *Sulfuric Acid.*

Billions of dollars' worth of liquefied cocaine were in each one, and would net Javi, his brother, sister, and ChaCha more money than Michael Jordan, Lebron James, Shaquille O'Neal and Kobe Bryant combined.

Javi, and ChaCha got hooked up to the propane trailers, while Evelyn and Xavier got coupled with the liquid chemical bulk tankers. Neither of them took any part of getting coupled up properly for granted. Too much was at stake to cut corners.

At the end of getting hooked up, Javi was checking all his wheels and tires on when Tool stepped up with Jamaica.

Tool was looking like he was ready to hit the club, rocking Balenciaga from head to toe, with a rose-gold Cartier on his wrist, and two long rose-gold Cuban link chains hanging from his neck. Jamaica looked like he was ready for the battlefield. He was dressed in a black hoody, black cargo pants with white and gray army fatigue prints and had black steel-toe boots on his feet.

"Rude bwoi! Whag'wan, tiguere!" the old school Jamaican said to Javi, embracing with an uncle-like hug.

"Jamaica, Jamaicaaaaa!" Javi sang out, making his voice raspy to imitate the King of the Marley family.

"Ya' already know, young one! Ready to help make 'de midwest's summa' feel like 'de winta'!"

"Yessir! We *tippin' the scales* in our favor once again!" Javi said, ready to see more zeros in his private account.

Nodding in agreement, Jamaica dapped Javi up once more, then he left and went to check up on Xavier and Evelyn.

"¿Qué lo qué, cabrón?" Tool said in his deep raspy voice as he dapped with Javi.

"Waka Flocka Flaaaame!" Javi joked, since so many people said Tool was like a Dominican/Puerto Rican version of the rapper, due to their uncanny looks.

Tool shook his head. "Here you go with that other shit," he said, then chuckled.

"Man, you know that's yo' twin brother, just like how people think me and Macho are brothers more than Xavier and I are because of how we both handsome light-skinned niggas with colored eyes."

Tool laughed. "I hear that hot shit, lil' nigga. Let's get ready to go. Time is money, B.

With their trailer inspections done, Javi, Xavier, Evelyn, and ChaCha were ready to go. As a necessity for if one of their trucks broke down, which was *not* good to be sitting on the side of any road with so much product, Tool was driving his big wrecker. In their H2s, the dread heads were ready to make sure every drop of each load made it to Illinois. They were all prepared to go to war with anyone foolish enough to even cross the street at the wrong time.

Chapter 9
XXXX

Back in, Winthrop Harbor, Illinois

Drunk and high as a kite, Creeper laughed his ass off at the faces of the four men around the table. They all looked pissed off. Losing ten grand shooting dice would make anyone upset.

They were sitting around a big table with a black tablecloth on it. Liquor and cocaine were on every damn near every surface, at his one-level home that looked modest from the outside, but inside, it was decked out all the way. The amount of money Creeper made off moving drugs for the Rojas-Gomez Cartel, doing it up to make it rival the luxury of a small mansion was nothing for him.

They were all *Norteños*, originally from Oakland, California. They'd developed a reputation for wet-work and kicking doors in, for the right price. The prince of the Rojas-Gomez cartel had heard of them during a trip out to visit some clients and ended up offering Creeper a position as an enforcer for his organization, in Illinois. The money that Creeper was offered to make the move was *waaaay* too much to pass up, so he hollered at his homies and a day later, they were in the Midwest.

Creeper was a tall light-brown skinned man, with a skinny build, and covered in tribal tattoos. His head was shaved, and it was tattooed as well. He looked like a tatted-up demon, due to the devil horns inked onto his forehead.

Along with Creeper and his clique, there were five very beautiful Mexican girls, all of them in tight sexy dresses, heels, hair and makeup did up, and they all smelled like candy. They were there for one reason, and one reason only: *to fuck.*

Corridos music blared from the big home audio system in the living room, all tributes to the boss of the Rojas-Gomez, competition of the Sinaloa Cartel.

A celebration was in effect. The previous week, Creeper and his guys had received their monthly shipment from the cartel. They had a few hundred kilos of Colombian cocaine, pure heroin straight from Vietnam, Mexican crystal meth, PCP, fentanyl, and boxes of prescription opioids that one could put Walgreens out of business. They'd already sold more than half of their stock and had over a million cash bundled and plastic wrapped, ready to be picked up and shipped back to Mexico.

With a huge cache of automatic guns and ammunition, all compliments of a few individuals in the Mexican Special Forces that didn't mind taking money to get them the firepower what they wanted, Creeper and his men had *no* worries at all.

"Yeeaaahh motherfuckers! Wooo!" Creeper teased, shouting as he stood up from his chair, holding up the winnings from the last hand. "I told y'all nobody can beat me! I do this shit, homes! Keep trying me and Imma take y'alls bitches too!"

His right-hand man, Baby Los, tall and skinny with long hair, his ponytail braided all the way down to his lower back, waved Creeper off.

"Whatever, dog. You wavin' the cash around like you ready to quit 'n shit. Why don't you sit down, vato, and get ready for another hand, eh?"

"Yeah, homes!" agreed Spider, an evil-looking man with brown skin, muscular physique from nearly six years in San

91

Quentin, and a low-faded haircut. "You doing all that talkin 'n shit, vato! Let's go! Stop stalling, carnal!"

The other two of Creeper's men, Dopey, shorter, fair-skinned, with a slicked back hairstyle, and Tarzan, tall, very skinny, brown, with long hair that touched his shoulders, were ready to try their luck again, but weren't feeling exceptionally optimistic about it. They both leaned forward to the table and snorted two big lines of coke each, trying to hype themselves up for the next hand, then they tossed back shots of tequila.

"Aight, aight, aight!" said Creeper, looking at his homies with a smirk. "Y'all fools wanna' lose more money, eh? Fuck it! Now, we shootin' for $500, so put up or shut up. ¡*Vamonos*, cabrones!" he said, then looked over at where the ladies were in the adjoining living room, snorting coke, taking shots, laughing as they partied amongst themselves. "Aye, chula!!" he shouted to the one with the gold hair, skimpy blue dress and silver pumps. "Ven aca and blow on these dice!"

The girl happily obeyed, hurrying over to the table as Creeper picked the dice up. He lowered his hand so the significantly shorter woman could blow on them. Opening his hand, she blew, then she looked up at him with a smile.

"Good job. When I break these fools' pockets again, I got something else I want you to blow on, aight?"

"I can't wait," she told him, then turned to leave.

Creeper smacked her petite little ass as she stepped off, making her shriek but smile.

He held the dice up and started shaking them up. "Aight, motherfuckers! Y'all asked for it!" he said, getting ready to throw them. "Here we goo!!"

KNOCK KNOCK KNOCK KNOCK!

Sudden knocking on the door halted him seconds before he shot the dice, pissing him off. His guys all looked at the front door, hands ready to reach for the AK-47s they all had leaning against their seats. The girls stopped partying and looked at the door, then back at the guys.

"¡Que chingao!" Creeper shouted. "Dopey! Go see who the fuck has the balls to knock on my shit and show up unannounced! If it's the cops, *blast they asses,* fool!"

Dopey obeyed and made his way to the door, taking a second to look out of the peephole. When he saw who was there, a gigantic grin grew on his face.

After he unlocked the two heavy-duty dead-bolt locks, the chain lock, and the standard door locks, Dopey opened the door up and nearly salivated over the gorgeous chick standing there, with a hand on her hip, striking an overly sexy pose.

With her hair styled to look wet, she was looking *too* damn good in her leather bustier, leather mini-skirt, and leather knee-high stiletto boots. Dopey's dick grew hard and started throbbing in his boxers.

Eeeeeeeee, Creeper's neice is so fucking bad, dog! I should fuck this little bitch and get her pregnant, just because he took my money, he thought to himself.

"Aye, man, what the fuck, joe?" the girl said impatiently. "You finna move outta my way or what, porky?"

Dopey smiled at her and stood aside. "My bad, chula. Come on in; we getting it poppin' in here."

She twisted her lips and stepped in, ignoring him. He was about to close the door when he saw her little brother coming. Right away, after remembering things he had heard about the young buck, Dopey curled his lip up in disgust, as if the youngster stunk.

Closing the door when the long-haired boy was in, Dopey re-locked all the locks. He heard, "Aaayyee! ¡Mi familia estan aqui" Creeper announced, hands up high, welcoming them in. "Magali! Mikey! Bring y'alls little asses over to uncle Creeper and snort some of this fucking yayo!"

Magali smirked as she led Mikey over to the table, ignoring the eyes of the other girls and Creeper's guys. She gave her uncle a hug, then grabbing a $100 dollar bill off the table, rolled it up and snorted two fat lines of coke quick.

She threw her head back and shrieked as the powdery drug took effect instantaneously. The sour-tasting backdrop numbed her throat. She closed her eyes and savored the feeling. Her pussy got moist and started thumping, craving some dick. She wished Stacks was there.

Mikey dapped his uncle up and snorted up some coke with another big face. Creeper's guys were all stuck, ogling Magali in that tight little skirt, wishing they could see what she had on under it.

"Damn, shortie," said Tarzan, licking his lips at Magali. "You grew up, eh?"

"Shortie?" Magali turned and looked at him with disdain. "First off, I ain't no muthafuckin' shortie, *homes*," she mocked. "I'm from Little Village, joe; with me, it's *King love* or *no love*, bitchass nigga!"

All of Creeper's guys started whooping and hollering, teasingly at her.

"Daaaaaaamn, homes, your niece dun' turned into a frosted flake, vato!" said Dopey, chuckling at his own joke.

Magali was about to snap when Creeper spoke up for her.

"Aye, homes, watch your fucking mouth!" he demanded, shooting a glare so venomous at the man that Dopey immediately shut up talking. 'This is my niece, pendejo. She can represent whatever clique she wants to, eh. Got it?!"

"Simon, carnal. My bad, dog," Dopey replied.

Lame-ass, Mikey thought to himself, staring at Dopey with hatred for him.

"Good," said Creeper. "Now... *lets turn the fuck up! Party time homes!"*

He grabbed the shot glass of Patron and was about to down the shot....

BOOOM!

The front door exploded with a loud blast. Pieces of wood and steel flew everywhere. Creeper, his guys, and the girls all jumped, completely startled by the loud explosion.

As they looked towards the smokey area, they all saw two men wearing masks run in. The tallest one carried a Draco with a drum; the shorter one had a sawed-off shotgun. Dopey tried to go for his AK and blast one of them but was too slow.

The shorter of the two saw him and pointed the 12-gauge at him. He pulled the trigger and blew Dopey's head off. His brains and skull fragments flew all over the place.

Tarzan, Spider, Baby Los, went for their guns but were also too slow. The shorter guy blew them all down with his Draco. Creeper, frozen in fear, stood where he was.

The girls screamed in fear, panicking, one of them pissing on themselves, another one of them started hyperventilating.

Creeper then noticed that only the girls were screaming, not his niece, nor his nephew. He turned his head and looked at them. He saw that they were both smirking at him. It then hit him… he'd been set up.

"Motherfuckers!" he growled, ready to strangle them.

With the two masked men walking up to Magali's and Mikey's side, Mikey pulled out a Glock 9 from his waistline and cocked it, pointing it at his uncle. Creeper immediately took off running for the kitchen, desperate to get to the rear door, which was his only way to get to safety.

He got to the rear door, hurried to unlock all the extra locks and yanked the door open, ready to run.

CRACK!

A wood Louisville Slugger came flying into his right knee completely destroyed his kneecap. Creeper screamed in agony from the pain. He hit the ground and grabbed his obliterated knee.

"Fuuucckkk!" he cried out as he rocked around on the ground.

Over his screaming he heard footsteps. He opened his eyes and saw a dark-skinned man with a bald-fade haircut, a red bandana covering his mouth, standing over him. In his hand, was the bat that had just fucked him up.

"*Daaaaaaaayuuuuuuum*, joe! I know that shit *had* to hurt!" Creeper heard the guy say, just before the man busted out laughing at him.

***

STACKS

He lowered the bandana that concealed his mouth and continued laughing at Creeper as the man cried. Rambo emerged from the kitchen and saw the shot-caller on the ground. He started laughing at his guy, seeing the bat in Stack's hand.

"Outta all the guns we got, lord, yo' ass wanna' use a muhfuckin' bat to get on dude," he said.

Before Stacks could give a reply, they both heard screams come from inside.

BOC! BOC! BOC! BOC! BOC! BOC! BOC! BOC! BOC!

The gunshots repeatedly went off for nearly a minute and then there was silence.

"See," Stacks said to his guy. "I told you lil' mama and her lil' bro be on 'bidness, lord."

Rambo waved it off. "Maaaaan, yo' bitch a snake, fam, and I think her lil' brother a homo, joe. On 'erythang."

Stacks shook his head. "Now yo' ass really tweakin', bruh."

Magali came through the back door just then, with a Glock in her hand. "Aye, man! Fuck is y'all doin' out here?! Let's get this shit done before 5-0 comes!"

"Yes, ma'am," Stacks replied with a smile.

Rambo shook his head, ignoring her.

Stacks and Rambo grabbed the whimpering head-honcho up, not giving a fuck about him crying and pleading for a doctor.

"Shut cho' bitchass up, sewer rat!" Magali shouted at her uncle, before she swung her pistol at him and cracked him in his jaw. "This how it's finna go down! You finna give up all the merch that you got up in this muthafucka, or you die a very painful death! ¡¿Me entiendes, pinche pervertido?!"

Creeper looked his niece in the eyes and saw fire in them. He nodded his head yes, then he was dragged into the house.

Creeper was dragged all the way back into the living room. He gasped when he saw the dead bodies of his crew, and the girls. Blood was splattered all over, and body parts littered the floor. It smelled like blood and feces and gun powder.

Another man was in the living room, standing next to his nephew. When the guy took his mask off, Creeper saw that the guy was a white boy.

"What the fu-fuck, 'Gali?! Mikey?!" he snapped, lying next to Dopey's headless corpse.

Magali looked down at her uncle, curling her lip up at him. Mikey stood on the other side of him. Stacks, Rambo, and the white boy stood silently, waiting for the two to handle their business.

Mikey suddenly kicked his uncle hard on the side of the head. "¡*Puto*! I was a fucking kid, motherfucker!"

Magali kicked Creeper on the other side of his head and screamed, "¡PINCHE *PERVERTIDO*! ¡CHINGATE!"

Stacks and Rambo both furrowed their eyebrows as the two began angrily attacking their uncle, screaming and cursing him out in Spanish. Neither of the three men knew what was being said, but they all could figure out that the two siblings' uncle had did something to them.

BOC!

Magali fired a shot from her Glock, popping Creeper right in his ass crack. He screamed like a banshee, so high-pitched that Stacks and Rambo wondered how it was that the windows didn't break.

"Maldito enfermo!" she shouted as tears ran down her face. "¡Violastes mi hermano pequeño, hijo de puta!"

Rambo glanced over at his guy. Stacks' eyebrows were furrowed in confusion. The white boy frowned, pissed at whatever it is that had Magali so upset. He was digging her hard and wanted her to be his woman.

"I'm s-s-s-sorryy!" Creeper screamed as he held his bleeding ass.

"Fuck you! Fuck yoooouuu!" Magali cried, now taking aim at his head, finger wrapped around the trigger.

Stacks hurried over and stopped her. "Whoa, whoa, whoa, lil' mama. Hold up, joe. I know you got a bone to pick with dude, but we need to get that merch first."

Magali's nostrils flared as she somehow found enough restraint to fall back. Mikey, eyes red like a demon child's, wanted to blow his uncle's head off so badly. The nightmares he'd had for so long after his uncle constantly raped him when he was a kid, tearing him apart, taking away his manhood, and turning him into what he called a "*freak*". He wanted to shoot Stacks for stopping him from finally killing the man that had treated him like a fuck-puppet, so many years ago.

Stacks crouched down next to Creeper and spoke. "I'm guessin' you did some real foul shit to them by the way they gettin' on yo' ass. This is what's gon' happen; you gon' tell me where the dope, the cash, and the guns is, then we gon' drop yo' ass off at the ER so you can get a band aid. If you don't, I will go get a butter knife and tell yo' niece to cut yo' nose off and make you smell yo' own booty. You understand me?"

Creeper nodded his head as he felt his body growing cold from losing blood.

"You-You don't kn-kn-know who you're m-messin' with, homes," he stammered.

Stacks stood back up, raising his bat up, aiming over his head.

"Okay! Okay, okkaayyy! It's in the basement homes! In a metal cabinet!!" Creeper then shouted, seconds before his face got bruised up.

Stacks looked at Mikey. "You and Brandon go check it out. Hurry up, too."

Mikey did as he was told. Brandon stepped up to Magali, smiling at her.

"When we get this money, I'm buyin' you a ring, beautiful. It's you and me, shorty, right?"

She smiled back at him. "You know it, papi. Go get to it so we can go."

He left to catch up with Mikey. Magali rolled her eyes and glanced over at Stacks, who was snickering to himself. She looked at Rambo and curled her lip up when she saw him mean-mugging her.

You're next, bitch, she thought to herself, plotting evilly in her head against him.

"Ooooooweeee! Eeeeeeee, joe, we in the muthafuckin' house!" Stacks exclaimed, when he saw Mikey and Brandon carrying big duffel bags that looked very heavy. "What we got in them thangz, joe?"

"Fam, we got coke, dope, meth, pills, cash, and some guns!" Brandon replied, super geeked. "This is like a lick a muhfucka hit in one of them lame-ass Urban Novels!"

Stacks and Rambo chuckled.

"Aight, white boy. Take 'em out to the whip; we'll be right there," Rambo said.

"Yup. Come one, Mikey," Brandon said.

"Naw. He's stayin' here. I told *you* to go!" Rambo demanded. "Hurry up, joe!"

Brandon groaned but did as he was told. He wanted that spot on the team that Magali told him would be his, if he proved himself.

Still bleeding out, Creeper felt himself fading in and out of consciousness. His heart dropped when he saw all the merch he'd been holding for the cartel.

"O-k-k-kay, bro!" he managed to say to Stacks. "You g-g-got the sh-shit... please... t-t-take me to the ho-h-hospital!"

Stacks looked at Magali and her brother.

"Handle y'all biz'," he told them.

Creeper's eyes went wide with horror when he saw his niece and nephew raise their cannons and point them at his face.

"WAIT! N-"

BOC! BOC! BOC! BOC! BOC! BOC! BOC! BOC! BOC! BOC! BOC! BOC! BOC! BOC! BOC! BOC! BOC! BOC!

They both unloaded on him. Overkill was an *understatement*. Magali and Mikey blasted their uncle. They blew his dick off first, then opened his chest, and last, pushed his face in. He was unrecognizable as a human when their clips were empty.

Brandon ran back into the house after hearing the gun fire. He thought something went wrong and had his Draco ready to spit if Magali was hurt.

Seeing she was okay; he went to her. "The bags are loaded in, bae. Can we get outta here now?"

"Sure, papi chulo," she told him. "Lead the way."

Brandon turned and started for the door.

Magali raised her pistol and fired. A slug slammed into the back of Brandon's head, pushing his brains out of the front of his forehead through the gaping hole the Hollow Point left behind.

The white boy fell dead to the ground, blood pouring out of the hole.

"Good job, baby," Stacks told her, giving her ass a pat. "Now we can go. When the cops get here, they'll think it was some goofy white boys that did this and turned on one of their own."

He walked off, exiting the house. Rambo followed; Magali looked at him, half wanting to blow *his* brains out, too.

"Chill," said Mikey, quietly in her ear. "Not yet."

She nodded, getting control of herself. Together, they looked at their dead rapist uncle once more, then left out of the house to catch up with Stacks and Rambo.

Chapter 10
XXXX

"¡Jefe! They're going to exit the highway!" Hidalgo heard Ramirez shout through the 2-way radio. "It's gonna be easier to get them on a state route!"

The leader of the Mexican sicarios, Hidalgo Cervantes, was formerly Special Forces in the Mexican military. He was now a part of the Mexican Mafia and ran his own crew of killers. He only took jobs that had high payouts; he never failed.

Thirty of his men, including him, were bunched up inside six Chevy Tahoes and GMC Yukons. Every single one of them were armed to the T with automatic AR-15s, fitted with 100-round monkey-nut drums. They wore Kevlar vests to protect their bodies; each one of them were ready to execute their mission to put an end to the so-called *untouchable* Valdez posse and collect the massive bounty the Rojas-Gomez prince had put on Javier Valdez's head.

"Copy that, Ramirez," Hidalgo replied, sitting back in the Yukon driven by his right-hand man. "Keep your pace; we don't want them knowing we're here. The element of surprise is everything when it comes to jobs like this."

"10-4, boss. Keeping back," Ramirez replied.

Hidalgo sent the Rojas-Gomez prince a text, up-dating him on their status. A thumbs-up emojii was sent back as a reply, then another came, saying, '*No fuck ups!*'

Hidalgo put his phone up and relaxed in his seat. He remained calm, never letting himself get too excited, or else he'd lose focus. He and his men were ready to show the underworld who the *real* killers were.

***

JAVI

At a small fuel station/restaurant, just outside of Easton, PA, Javi and the convoy stopped to top off their fuel tanks and to take a little break.

As Javi started filling the tank on the driver's side, he peeped something that seemed odd to him. He watched and studied what he was seeing. Having been taught to never question his instincts, he opened his door and grabbed his iPhone off the charger and called ChaCha.

He told her what he had seen. ChaCha chuckled then responded back.

"Seen that a long time ago, papacito. No te apures," she told him. "Come on over here and talk to me. I have a plan that's gonna fuck heads all the way up."

Javi chuckled to himself as he ended the call. Turning back around and looking in the direction of where they'd gone and smirked to himself.

"I got somethin' for all you hoe-ass niggas," he said to himself. "Come on and bring it."

***

XXXX

"Alright, caballeros! Maintain your distance but get ready! We hit them hard, and fast! No mistakes!" Hidalgo shouted into his 2-way, after he and his crew followed the Valdez convoy off the main interstate, now on a county route that was so far away from 78 and desolate that it wasn't even on the map.

Hidalgo saw the perfect opportunity arising to get the mission done; nothing but farmland and pitch-black skies were around.

A little further up the road, Hidalgo gave the word to commence. "Okay! Ramirez! Zapata! *Go! Go! Go! Take the last hummer out first!*"

Ramirez and Zapata gunned their engines and broke formation. They both swerved into the on-coming lane, speeding up to catch the rear Hummer.

In front of Zapata, Ramirez and the five men in his Tahoe eagerly sat straight up, ready to get it on, when suddenly, as Ramirez ran up alongside the big tow truck, the driver of it swerved to the left and smacked into the Tahoe so hard that it careened out of control.

Ramirez tried to counter-steer, but was unable to, and lost control and ran right into a tree. The Tahoe exploded on impact, turning into a big fire ball.

Hidalgo cursed as the Yukon he was in flew past the burning SUV. He shouted to Zapata to take the tow truck out.

Two men riding on the passenger's side of Zapata's SUV hung out the windows and started firing their guns. The Hummer that was in front of it swerved out from behind the last semi. The rear window dropped down and bullets began firing from inside.

The windshield of Zapata's Tahoe exploded as bullets flew through it. He took three to the face before the top of his head was blown off. The shooter in the front passenger's seat tried to grab the wheel and gain control before they crashed, but from the Hummer, a grenade came flying right through the window.

BOOM!

The Tahoe exploded, flying up and off the road, landing sideways on the side of the road.

The third and fourth SUVs' occupants got nervous, but with their boss yelling at them to start shooting, they hung out of their windows and started shooting at any of the vehicles that they could.

The third Yukon got past the tow truck and ran right up on the Hummer, but the Hummer swerved back in front of the tow truck.

A dance ensued with the tow truck swerving to get behind the Yukon. The semi then swerved to stay in front of the Yukon. As soon as the semi driver was where they needed to be they slammed on their brakes. The Yukon's driver tried to follow suit, but it was too late, and he slammed into the back of the semi-truck.

The tow truck then rammed the Yukon from behind and started pushing on it, while the semi in front kept its brakes on. The men inside panicked as the two trucks started crushing the Yukon, with them inside of it. The three men in the back of the Yukon turned around and saw the silhouette of the tow truck's driver move, just before a flicker of light came. The next thing they knew, a grenade was inside with them.

BOOM!

The tow truck pushed the burning SUV off the road when the semi in front let off the brakes and pulled away.

The fourth SUVs' occupants had no clue what to do.

"¡Jefe¡ ¡¿Que vamos hacer?!" Armando shouted through the 2-Way from the front passenger's seat.

"¡Matalos! Kill that fucking tow truck driver!" Hidalgo shouted back.

Armando and his guys didn't even get the chance. The tow truck's rear boom lowered down right in front of them. The driver tried to stop, but it was no use. A flame produced from a custom gas-line inside the stinger ignited and shot under the SUV. The flame reached the rear of the SUV, hitting the fuel tank.

BOOM!

"¡Chingao!" shouted Hidalgo as the last of his men fried to death.

"Boss, we can't get them!!" shouted Leonardo, the driver of Hidalgo's Yukon. "We gotta get outta here!"

"¡Si, si, si! Stop and turn around!" Hidalgo agreed.

Leonardo hit the brakes, bringing the Yukon to a screeching halt. The three men in the back flew forward from the abrupt stop. The trucks sped away, not a single brake light coming on.

Whipping the wheel to the left, Leonardo got the Yukon turned around and mashed the gas. He gunned it back the way they came, racing to get far, far away before state troopers began showing up.

He passed all four wrecked SUVs that now had the skeletal remains of their crew inside, still burning to a crisp.

Up ahead, Hidalgo saw something that made his eyes go wide in shock. He cursed when he saw a Cadillac Escalade blocking the road, and posted on the side of it, was the Valdez posse, with a huge dog, that he thought he and his men were chasing. And they were all holding assault rifles, pointing right at Hidalgo's SUV.

"How in the fuck are they there!" Leonardo screeched as he slammed on the brakes, skidding the Yukon to a stop, about a hundred feet away from the mob.

"Reverse! Reverse! Get us outta here!" Hidalgo yelled, grabbing his AR-15 to start firing.

Leonardo hurried to put it in reverse. He mashed the gas pedal to the floor... but the Yukon didn't move.

Suddenly, bright lights filled the Yukon from behind. They all turned and saw that the big tow truck was right behind them, blocking them from getting out of there.

***

JAVI

Javi, Xavier, Evelyn, and ChaCha, with Pablo at her side, advanced on the Yukon with their fully automatic *H&K G36s* with red-beam sights, trained on the windshield. Tool hopped out of his tow truck with an automatic AA12 shotgun, equipped with a 25-round drum, loaded with incendiary shells.

Like a trained military squad, the Valdez posse positioned themselves at the front, sides, and rear of the Yukon, and waited. ChaCha and Pablo stood at the front, her laser pointing right at the driver's face.

Javi, at the driver's window, yelled for the man to roll the window down. The driver complied, scared shitless.

"Don't shoot! Don't shoot!" he pleaded with his hands up.

At the front passenger's side window, Xavier had his G36 trained on the boss, while his sister had the left rear, and Tool had the right rear.

"Get the fuck out the truck, bitch!" ChaCha roared, as Pablo growled, licking his chops hungrily.

"Okay! Okay! Just...don't shoot!" the driver shouted.

He and the men in the rear got out with their hands up. Evelyn and Tool quickly relieved them of their guns. The man in the front passenger's seat, though, remained.

"What's wrong, homeboy?" Xavier asked him with a smirk on his face. "You piss yo' pants and don't wanna get out for us to clown yo' dumbass about it?"

The man looked at him with a venomous stare. "¡*Chingate*, puto!" he spat.

BRRRRRRRRRRRRRRRRRRRRRRRRRRRRRRRRRRRRRRR!

Xavier squeezed the trigger and blew the man to pieces. "Fuck *you*, bitch," he then said, replying to what the Mexican had just said to him in Mexican-dialect Spanish.

The others started panicking when they saw the man ended up in bloody chunks, all over the inside of the Yukon.

"That must've been y'alls boss, huh?" Javi asked the driver.

The driver nodded. "Y-Yeah, m-m-man! Please! We were j-just doing our job! It's not p-personal!"

"Not personal?" he asked with a raised eyebrow.

BOOM!

Tool blew the gauge and took the head of one of the men that got out of the driver's side clean off.

The driver started crying then.

BRRRRRRRRRRRRRRRRRRRRRRRRRR!

Down went another man.

BRRRRRRRRRRRRRRRRRRRRRRRRRRRRRRR!

And another.

BOOM! BOOM! BOOM! BOOM! BOOM!

All that was left was the driver. Stricken with fear, the man's bowels evacuated.

"I'ma ask you just one time," Javi said to him, pointing the red dot right at the driver's forehead. "Victor Gomez sent you, yeah?"

The driver nodded his head.

"Thought so," Javi said, then squeezed the trigger, painting the side of the Yukon crimson with the driver's blood. "You snitched, bitch, so you had to die."

ChaCha chuckled at the young green-eyed goon. "Okay, y'all. Let's get up outta here. Our window with the PA State Troopers is closing fast," she said, just as headlights shone on them.

They all looked and saw a state trooper SUV creeping towards them. ChaCha walked up to the driver's window with her dog right at her side. The trooper that was behind the wheel rolled the window down and looked at the bloody mess.

"Have fun," she told him, with a smirk.

Without another word, she and Pablo got into the Escalade. Javi hopped up front with ChaCha and Evelyn got in back. Xavier jumped up into the tow truck with Tool. Together they all dipped off, racing to catch up with their trucks, driven by Jamaica and his goons. The trooper waited for ten minutes after their taillights could no longer be seen, then called in the gruesome scene, claiming to have seen a gang of white men on hogs raced past him, going towards the New Jersey state line.

"Yooooo, pullin' the switcheroo on them pussy muhfuckas was dope as fuck, cuzzo!" Javi said to ChaCha, as she gunned the Escalade's engine. "Why didn't I think of that?"

"Because I am la ChaCha, and I do this shit, baby boy," she replied with a smile. "Now get your head back in mode; we still gotta get back to Illinois with the loads. After we get to Joliet, you can relax."

Javi nodded, then looking down at his gun, he smiled. "I am *soooo* glad bae got me this muthafucka! This bitch is getting' dipped in gold and goin' on the mantle over my fireplace!"

Chapter 11
STACKS

A little after 7 o'clock in the morning, Stacks, Rambo, Magali, and Mikey, stood in the kitchen of Rambo's crib, out in North Chicago, also known as *NOGO*, a town right next to Waukegan. They all stood completely still, straight stuck at the sight of what sat on the table in front of them.

Stacked up on the table, was sixty bricks of cocaine, fifty bricks of heroin, thirty kilos of crystal meth, twenty-five kilos of fentanyl, five big jars filled with Oxycontin, and two 5-gallon buckets full of PCP.

Sitting on the floor was two big duffel bags full of cash that hadn't even been counted out yet; one filled with pistols, choppers, and a few shotguns, and one with all sorts of ammunition.

It had just sunk in, the lick they hit, being real. Shit like that only happened in farfetched Urban Novels. Who hit stains and made come ups like that?

"Holy shit... Lord... yo' ass *wasn't* cappin', joe," Rambo said, still stuck in disbelief.

"This is crazy," Magali said then.

Mikey stood silent, looking at the cocaine, his mouth watering as if he was looking at candy.

Stacks took a deep breath to contain his excitement. This was the lick he'd been waiting for since he learned what a lick was. He was now rich, and *nobody* in *his* crew died.

"Aight. Okay," he said, gathering himself up to be the boss. "First and foremost, we not movin' *none* of this shit out here. We can pop a little bit off in Zion, and up in Keno and Racine, even Milwaukee, but I'm sendin' most of this shit down to the city, joe."

"I can handle that," Magali volunteered. "I know a lot of people in my hood, and all the other hoods. 26th and Cal gon' eat what I bring up, then I can drop some in Crown Town, and maybe even in Humboldt Park."

"I can make some moves out Willy," Rambo then said, knowing exactly who he would hit with some of the dope and coke.

Stacks shook his head. "Naw, Lord. I'ma let the lil' Lords come grab and take down. Let them work while we collect, you dig I'm sayin'?"

Rambo nodded.

Still quiet, Mikey was only thinking about how high he was going to be getting. He was so anxious to snort some coke that his dick got hard.

"What about you, shorty?" Stacks asked him just then.

Mikey looked at him. "I'm wherever you need me to be," he replied, trying to hide the itch he was feeling.

Stacks nodded his head, though Rambo looked at him with a peculiar expression. Magali looked at Rambo with furrowed eyebrows.

"Say less. Rambo, call the lil' guys and get 'em up here. I know some young Lords up in the Mil' that I'ma call and have ride down. Magali, grab what you gon' need and go on ahead down. Mikey, you stand by. What I'ma have you do is hold on to some things, that way 'erythang ain't all here. Shit happens, and it's best to spread out."

Mikey hid the smile that wanted to explode on his face and nodded. Magali nodded her head as well, rubbing her hands together at the same time, ready to get money.

"Can I have some coke for myself?" Mikey asked Stacks.

111

Stacks looked at the young one. "Yeah. Take a whole thang for 'yoself. You earned it, but don't get too reckless."

With lightning-fast speed, Mikey ran to the table, grabbed a brick, and pulling out a hunting knife from his pocket, he flipped the blade out and jabbed it into one of the bricks of coke.

His sister shook her head and watched as he made a hole big enough to scoop some out. He pushed one nostril closed, then with the other one that was still open, he put the little mound to it and inhaled.

"Wooooo! Shiittt!" he squeaked, throwing his head back as the blissful sour-tasting drip oozed down his throat, numbing it instantly.

Now the real Mikey is gonna come out, Magali thought to herself, knowing how her little brother got when he was geeking from cocaine.

Stacks and Rambo busted out laughing as he snorted another bump.

"Aight, Mikey, damn!" his sister snapped, walking up to him and stopping him from doing more. "Chill the fuck out! Yo' ass be getting way too damn loose with that shit, dude!"

"Bitch, shut up! I *earned* this shit! You heard what Stacks said!"

"Mike-Mike, listen to yo' sister, joe. She just tryna make sure that yo' ass don't overdose," Stacks said.

"I gotta make a run, joe," Stacks said to Rambo. "You in charge, Lord."

"Why him?" Magali protested.

"Because I'm *big homie*, shortie," Rambo told her, daring her to get buck.

"Aye, man, chill out!" Stacks interrupted, before shit got crazy between the two. "We just came into some serious wealth... *together!* Don't fuck this up by lettin' childish animosity fuck it up!"

Magali smacked her lips. "Whatever, *Stacks!*"

Stacks went and stepped to her, looking down at the beautiful chicana. "You back talkin' me, shortie? You need me to put somethin' in yo mouth to make you shut it the fuck up?"

Magali licked her lips seductively. "Yeah, I do."

Without another word, Stacks took her hand and pulled the little freak out of Rambo's kitchen, to one of his guest bedrooms, slamming the door shut.

Rambo chuckled to himself. He heard snorting behind him a second later. Turning, he saw Mikey was snorting more of the coke.

"Don't kill 'yoself, lil' dude," he said, but was really thinking, *Gon' ahead and overdose, you little bitch. I'ma kill you and yo' thot-ass sister anyways.*

Mikey looked at him and smiled.

You's a fuckin' weirdo, Rambo then thought, just as the sounds of moaning and groaning came from the guest bedroom.

Ignoring it, he got on business. He got his phone out and made the calls to all the young Vicelords from his and Stacks' hood, telling them to get up to NOGO right now.

Mikey took a brick of white gold and put it in a plastic shopping bag. "I'll be back later, joe," he told Rambo.

"Fuck is you goin'?"

"To my crib. I need a shower, and I got shit to do," Mikey said, then without another word, he scurried out of the house and hopped into his black 2003 Chevy Trailblazer, dipping off like he had to get to the bank before it closed.

From the window, Rambo watched the little geek monster speed off down the street. A red flag immediately went off inside of his head. He just knew that Mikey was going to do some stupid shit and end up getting caught up with the coke. Rambo had been around the block and knew that Mikey was the type that if he got caught up by the jakes, he would most definitely tell to get up out of that jam.

Making a mental note, Rambo vowed to keep a very close eye on Mikey. The first sign of him bringing danger to him, or his bro and it would be curtains for the young coke fiend.

Rambo then went back into the kitchen and started sorting what he was giving the youngsters from the hood, what he was letting Magali take, and what he was going to stash. He then grabbed the duffel bag with the money. His eyes lit up when he saw so many big faces. Never had he seen so much cash all at one time. He figured there had to be at least $100 grand in it.

He grabbed five big bundles of the gwap and put it in a cupboard, stashing them in a box of Cheerios. He was zipping the bag up when the sounds of Magali screaming and crying out Stacks' name got even louder. He paused, dick getting hard as he started picturing his own bitch riding his dick. He pulled his phone back out and made a call.

"Hey, papi," answered Carmen.

The sound of his Bolivian baby momma excited him. "What up? Where you at?"

"At home with yo' daughter."

"I'm finna ride through in a few and drop some shit off for y'all," he told her.

She giggled. "What else you gonna drop off, baby?" she asked with sexual undertones.

"Ten inches of hard Black dick in that wet-ass Spanish pussy," he told her.

"Ay, Dios mio, papi vente ahora mismo," she told him.

"Whatever you said, say that shit when I get there. Love you."

"I love you, too, papi. Te veo muy pronto."

***

VICTOR

Fuming as he sat in his deluxe presidential office, Victor was more livid than he could ever remember being before in his life. One thing he was pissed about was how he'd just received the news about one of his dope houses being hit up, and everyone inside had been murdered gruesomely. The man he had in charge of the house had been decapitated. When the cops arrived, they found the man's headless corpse laying on its stomach, pants down, head placed so that his own face was in his ass crack.

What he hadn't received was a call from *Hidalgo*, telling him that the Valdez convoy had been stopped, and that they were all dead. The call he *did* received about it, was from a law enforcement ally, informing him that Hidalgo, and his men, were all dead.

He ground his teeth as he saw nothing but red. He knew his father would be calling, very soon, and would no doubt spazz on him. Even though his father barely ever left Mexico, the man knew everything, sometimes before anything even happened. He had a lot of eyes in law enforcement that belonged friends, and family.

Across from his desk, was an older, brown-skinned man, with long black hair pulled back into a ponytail, a hard face that had a scar from the left eyebrow, down to his cheek. He was a little taller than average, and in very good shape for a guy that was in his early 50s.

The look on his face said that he wasn't happy about being rushed from Matamoros, where he'd been living it up with beautiful women, to Waukegan, to help Victor get at people that he'd been warned about screwing with, for a very long time.

The man went by the name *Diablo*. He was reported to be pure evil, and nothing less.

"I don't appreciate having to cut my vacation short, Vic," the man rasped. "I had the baddest chulitas on my dick at home, good tequila, and good cocaine. I had to leave all that behind just to come help you put an end to whom everyone that tried before has failed? ¡*No mames*, güey!"

Victor shook his head. "It's *my* fucking money that got you those little bitches, that good tequila and it's *my* good coke that you're snorting! Oh, don't forget that it's my money that got you living in that big-ass house in Matamoros, and down in Sinaloa! So, when I call, you fucking jump! ¡¿Comprendes?!"

"Suuuure, I understand," Diablo replied sarcastically. "So, what do you have planned that may miraculously do the trick of getting rid of these...............kids?"

Victor could hear the sarcasm but chose to ignore it. "First, find out who the fuck hit my spot up and killed Creeper and his crew. Those motherfuckers took everything, and I want their fucking heads! Barrera said there were women there, too, which Creeper knew that was a no-no. There was a guero there that he said was not part of Creeper's crew, so it had to be some clown-ass white boys that hit my shit."

"Or," Diablo said, pondering what he was hearing. "The white boy could be a decoy to throw off the scent of your bloodhound."

"How do you mean?" Victor asked.

"Barrera called me, too, knowing that you were calling me in," said Diablo. "The guero had a shotgun and the pinche pig said it was what took off one of Creeper's guy's heads and hit a few others. But the gunshots discovered in the others, didn't come from his gun. So, there were others. I think the white boy was a send-off, and he ended up getting sent off to meet his maker."

Victor nodded his head, agreeing with the logic. "That still doesn't say that it wasn't gueros that did this, but what we can look for, is movement on the streets."

Diablo agreed. "Las calles hablarán, güey."

"Yes, they will, and when they do, you will have your guys scope out everyone moving my shit. Follow them and see who they're copping from, then snatch them up and torture the *fuck* out of them! Make them cry like bitches! Make it *hurt*!"

Diablo nodded. "Anything else?"

"Yeah! Change that dumbass name you go by! Diablo, though? Come on, vato! Who the fuck goes by some dumb shit like that?!" Victor busted out laughing at the man. "You should just let people call you Machete, because you look just like Dany Trejo!"

Diablo gave an unenthused chuckle, then thought to himself, *Your whores like my name just fine, pendejo*

"Thanks," he said instead. "Hey. Where's that secretary of yours, eh? I could use a little coffee."

Victor shot up out of his chair and snapped. "Get out! ¡Largate de mi oficina! Take your old ass to Dunkin' Donuts and get some coffee!"

Diablo laughed at him, then took his leave. Victor hit a button on the intercom phone on his desk, calling the new secretary that replaced his old one.

"Penelope! I need you in here now!" he demanded.

Less than a minute later, the 5'2" Guatemalan woman entered his office. She was a beautiful lady with skin the color of mocha. Her long silky wheat-colored hair was flat-ironed and hung loosely down her shoulders. She wore black eyeliner, red lipstick, a red form-fitting dress that had a low cleavage line, and a below mid-thigh-length hem. On her little feet, she had on nude-colored pumps with pointed toes and 5" heels.

Victor had hired her just the day before. Out of all the other choices, he'd gotten word from one of his terminal supervisors that a woman had been making daily calls and showing up every day, looking for a job. He arranged to interview her, and the second he saw her, he wanted her, literally.

He hired her on the spot, after he got a sample what skills she *really* possessed.

117

"¿Si, Señor Gomez?" she said, with a sweet and innocent voice.

Victor stood up and smiled at her, undoing the button to his pants. "Chula, ven y ponte este chile en tu boca de nuevo como lo hiciste antes," he told her as he freed his hard cock, wagging it at her.

The woman smiled at him, then closed and locked the door behind her. "Con plaser, jefe," she purred, then strutted over to him, dropping to her knees before him, and opening her mouth wide for him to put his dick in her mouth.

It feels sooooo good to be the boss! WOOOO! Victor thought to himself, as the beautiful woman sucked his hard cock like she was auditioning for a role in a porn hub flick.

Chapter 12
JAVI

Making it back to Murrysville, Javi, his brother, sister, ChaCha, Tool, and the Rastas all went to the PJ&D yard to re-group. A call ahead from ChaCha had a mob of security guards meet them right outside of the turnpike and follow them back to the yard. When they arrived, there were so many armed men there that it looked like Kim Jong Un had been called in to train them all.

They fueled their trucks up, ChaCha walking Pablo while her tanks were filled; once topped off, they rode over to the wash ports and cleaned their rides, then went to park.

After a good meal, they all headed up to their rooms in the PJ&D hotel to get some rest and re-charge for the remainder of the trip home.

Right as he was trying to fall asleep, Javi got a call from Angela. He forwarded her to voicemail, then passed out on the big comfy bed.

***

CHACHA

"Yes, Diesel, we're good, papi," she told him, answering the question that the Valdez family's boss had asked when she answered his call.

Laying on her bed with Pablo at her side, ChaCha was ready to close her eyes and drift right off, when he called her. Despite how tired she was, she lit up when she saw the number to his burner phone that he kept in his prison cell.

"I saw them clowns comin' a mile away," she continued. "They followed us all the way from by *my* yard."

She heard Danny groan and curse. "Yo, why you let that happen? You could've had Jamaican 'n 'nem *ta-dow* on they ass *waaaay* sooner than that, ma."

ChaCha giggled. "I know. But where's the fun in that?"

"Movin' a few billion dollars' worth of white doesn't require fun, Ximena. Come on now, ma."

She sighed. "You're right. I just… there's no excuse for what I allowed to let happen. My word, yo, I won't let it get that far again, okay?"

"Cool. You all in the rooms now?"

"Yeah," ChaCha giggled again as Pablo moved his face and started licking her mouth.

"Why you gigglin' like that? Lemme find out, 'Mena."

"Find out what, Diesel?"

"That you got another man with you."

"I do," she told him.

"I'ma fuck you up. Pablo don't count."

ChaCha busted out laughing. "Then in that case, no, and never. Este chocha sólo se moja por *ti*, papi. Tú lo sabes."

Danny chuckled. "It better only get wet for me. Don't make me break up outta this joint to come kill one of them clown-ass niggaz that *think* he can get my chick."

"Don't even think like that, because if you break out, then we gotta go to Japan, or Morocco."

"Why there?" Danny asked.

"No extradition, and y cuando yo te tenga otra vez en mis brazos, no te dejaré ir. I promise you that."

"Listen to you. It sounds like you like me, bae," Danny joked.

"Naw, I do *not* like you, Diesel," ChaCha told him, with a smile as she stroked under her dog's chin. "I love you, baby."

She then heard Danny sigh.

"I love you, too, Ximena. Yo, do me a favor, though."

"Anything, mi amor," she swore.

"Make sure my lil' cousin has the best b-day bash ever, ma."

"I promise, bae. Word on my motha', he gon' leave out that bitch with a smile bigger than the Viagra man's."

Danny busted out laughing so hard that ChaCha couldn't help but laugh her ass off with him.

***

JAVI

A little after 8 o-clock that night, Javi woke up from his alarm beeping. He yawned and stretched, feeling refreshed and ready to hit the road. Checking his phone, he saw several missed calls, texts, and a variety of notifications. He looked at the notifications from nine of his drivers first. Logging into his e-mail account, he saw nine in his inbox. Clicking them, they included *Load Delivered* confirmation pictures.

Javi used what was called a *Factoring* company to get paid after every load delivered by one of his trucks was confirmed. How it worked was simple; his drivers, when they delivered a load, the person at the place receiving it, signed the Bill of Lading, then the driver took a picture of the signed documents, e-mailed the photo to Javi, then Javi forwarded the flicks to the factoring people. The signature was the proof they required to issue payment. They paid the price negotiated by the cargo's owner, and the trucking company, minus their small percentage. They then billed the cargo's owner for the full price. It worked for many truck company owners, because they got paid per load, instead of waiting for 30-40 days.

After forwarding the nine photos to the factoring people, Javi went into his business account and electronically deposited what he paid his drivers for their hard work, plus a bonus, while he waited for the factoring people to deposit the money into his business's account.

Next, he returned Michelle's call, before anything else.

"Are y'all okay, baby?" she asked upon immediately answering his call on the first ring.

"Yeah. We Gucci. You?"

"Claro, papi, but until you called me back, I *wasn't* cool, yo. News travels fast, and that shit is on every channel and Smart phone news app."

"Oh really? Any suspects?', Javi asked with a chuckle.

"The Chief of PA State Troopers announced that they believe a bunch of bikers had attempted to have it out with a rival biker gang."

Javi busted out laughing. "Hmmm. Big cuz a beast, yo."

Michelle chuckled. "She is. Everybody else is okay?"

"Yep. We about to hit it on back to the Illy. How much longer 'til you're done?"

"Um… a few more days," she said with a giggle.

"Why you hesitate like that?" he asked, suspicious of how her answer sounded.

"I don't know what you're talking about, bae."

"Uh huh. Lemme find out you took another job, Michelle."

"After holla'in at ya mans, then takin' care of that crooked-ass lawyer, then this, fuck no! I'ma be takin' a nice long vacation. But I do got some shit I'm plannin' as we speak."

"Like?"

"You'll see, Javi. I love you."

He smiled. "I love you, too, amor. Call me when you're comin' home."

"Why? So, you'll know when to pull ya' dick up outta that thot- bitch?"

"Michelle!"

She busted out laughing. "I'm just playin', Javier... or am I?"

"Yooooo, I'ma really kick yo' ass when you get back."

"Wanna bet that I have you doin' everything but that?"

"Shush. Te hablo despues, bae."

"Te amo mucho," Michelle told him again.

"I love you more," he replied, then ended the call before she could argue with him about that.

***

He took a quick shower and dressed in a work shirt with Dedicated Transport on the front, and a logo flick of his Kenworth on the back, 501 Levis jeans and Timberlands on his feet. Returning the rest of the calls he'd missed, except for Angela's.

He met everyone down in the restaurant and joined them for a plate of delicious Caribbean cuisine before they headed out to their trucks to go.

While pouring some engine oil into his engine's oil reservoir, Jamaica pulled up in his H2 Hummer, rolling his window down.

"Rude bwoi, ya good?" the ol' head Rasta asked.

"Yessir. Ready to get back home," Javi told him.

Jamaica nodded his head. "Me 'ear 'dat. Me and me shottaz make sure 'dat happens, no doubt, baby boy."

"I would never doubt you, tio," Javi swore.

***

Back on the road, ChaCha led the way onto the Turnpike. They all headed east, taking I-76 into Ohio, then the Ohio

Turnpike to Indiana. They took a break after pushing the 5-hour ride without stopping, then made it back into Illinois.

Still leading the convoy, ChaCha switched off the East-West Toll Road, and entering Illinois on I-80/90, finished the last leg of the trip to Joliet.

Arriving at *PJ&D Industries, Inc.*, they entered the massive cleaning chemical production factory created by Pedro Valdez, Javi's great uncle, that was now being ran by his other great uncle, Juanito, and his grandfather Diego. The enormous property was surrounded by tall barbwire fencing, and heavily armed ex-military soldiers. They all took their tanker trailers to a drain port in the rear, parked at one, and after hooking up the big suction hoses to the drain spouts on their trailers, they emptied every drop of liquid yayo into the underground storage tanks.

With their tankers empty, they took them to another PJ&D yard, in Romeoville, just west of Joliet and uncoupled from the tankers.

Javi was sitting in his seat, forwarding a few more e-mails from drivers to the factoring company, when he saw a notification for the deposit for the delivery of his load made to his private offshore account. Seeing *over* $165 million dollars added to the hundreds of millions of dollars he already had in it, Javi grinned like a homeless man that had just won the Powerball.

Before he pulled off, he went into the account and made several donations to charities for homeless and hungry children, animal rescue organizations, battered women shelters, cancer treatment facilities, and school systems.

In less than twenty minutes, he had donated just over half of what he had just gotten, and he didn't feel any attachment to a dime of it. Satisfaction to him, was doing good because he *could*, not to receive anything back.

Just then, he heard someone knocking at his door. He looked out of his window and saw his big muscular 6'1" Ox-built grandfather there.

"¡Oye, que pasoooooo, tigueraso!" Diego bellowed.

"Oh snap! Grandpa! ¡La bendicion!" Javi replied, extending respect to his grandfather the way he'd been taught to do from his childhood. Excitedly, he opened his door and jumped out of the cab, embracing the ol' head like he hadn't just seen him a week ago. "What are you doin' here, ol' head?"

"Had to check on you, young man," Diego told him. "I heard things got a little crazy in PA?"

"That Rojas-Gomez clown sent more shooters at us, but they failed," Javi stated.

"I can see that. We have a strong force with us," Diego reminded him, as Jamaica walked up and dapped his childhood best friend up. "You all are very resourceful as well, papa. Ximena told me about the trick you played on those payasos."

Javi chuckled.

"Me brudda, 'dem pussy-hole muddafuckaz neva' saw 'eet comin'," Jamaica chimed in, with a chuckle. "Me no unda'stand why 'dem bomba-clots keep tryin', but it's all good, 'mon. We'll keep killing 'dem."

Diego chuckled at his homie.

"Where's my g-ma at?" Javi asked his grandfather.

"Handling a little business with Carolina. She says she will see you soon, and Happy Birthday."

Javi nodded his head. "Thanks, ol' head."

"Yah, 'mon, happy birthday to ya, Javier," Jamaica added, dapping Javi up.

"Michelle won't be back for a few more days, grandpa, so you and grandma should come past the crib and keep me company for my b-day."

Diego started smiling. "Sure, Javier. Sounds good."

"Te hablo despues, Viejo," Javi then said, before climbing back up into this Large Car and pulling off, leaving the two O.G.s with smiles on their faces.

On the E-Way heading north, Javi got yet another call from Angela. Pissed that she kept calling, he answered this time.

"Yo, what up, man?" he asked angrily.

"¿Papi? ¿Donde estas ahora? ¡Te extraño!" she whined.

Javi groaned, shaking his head. "I'm on my way home, shortie. Why is you buggin' like this?"

"¡Por que yo quiero verte, Jabier! ¡¿Por que diablos no me llamaste cuando regresaste?! ¡He estado esperando que me llames!"

Javi suddenly grew furious at her questioning him. He snapped.

"Bitch! I don't gotta tell you shit! Who the fuck are you to question me? I run this shit! Fuck is wrong with you, pendeja?"

Angela started crying. "¡Jabier! ¿Por que me gritas?! ¡Solo quiero verte!" she told him.

"I don't give a fuck what you want, bitch! Stop fuckin' hittin' my line like yo' dumbass is crazy! You ain't my bitch, so stop tryna act like you are! ¿¡*Entiendes*, cabrona?!"

"S-S-Si, papi... I sorry!"

Javi ended the call on her. "Dumbass bitch. Fuck that hoe. It's a wrap," he said to himself, no longer wanting to cheat on the woman he loved more than life.

Chapter 13
XXXX

Out In Zion

Goooodamn! She so muthafuckin' thick! I should make that bitch buss' it open again for a nigga, joe. On the Five! he thought to himself, as he sat posted in his whip.

Having timed it just right, he saw her running out of the Wal-Mart as fast as the gold flats she had on would carry her. He had to admit, the simple Wal-Mart uniform she wore for her job as a cashier there was *still* sexy as shit! She had on the dark blue polo-style shirt, skin-tight beige leggings, and the metallic gold flats on her feet. Her fiery red hair was the color of blood. She was a bad, *bad* bitch, to say the least.

Thinking about all the times that he had enjoyed her *phenomenal* oral skills, and all the times he had beat the pussy up and hit it hard and fast from the back while he smacked on her voluptuously fat ass, damn near made him want her back. But she talked too much shit for him and he was *seriously* put off by her disease.

Knowing said disease was flaring up on her, he knew that and if she didn't get to a bathroom *very* soon... she'd be ruining yet *another* pair of panties.

He started laughing when he saw her cup her super fat and round ass with one of her hands. Starting his engine, he hurried up and pulled out of his spot, so he could be in position. He had a surprise for her.

CHRISTOPHER "DIESEL" HORNEZES

***

KENZIE

Kenzie, a statuesque 5'10" woman of Cuban and Armenian descent, cursed and groaned as she reached her clunker Toyota Corolla. Her bowels were threatening to burst. The pressure building inside of her gut hurt her so bad that she wanted to just push it all out, but she didn't have time to take a shower and change. Her lunch break was only a half an hour.

The embarrassingly pesky bowel disease she had was flaring up on her, again, at the worst time. Even though she'd taken her medication to help ease her Crohn's, flare-ups were still *very* common for her and often happened at the worst time possible. What was even worse was that she was a germaphobe. Kenzie was *terrified* to use a public restroom, even the one at her job. Her lunch break was her opportunity to use the bathroom at her 2-bedroom apartment, which was literally a 4-minute drive away from job.

Kenzie was blessed with an *amazingly* voluptuous body. Her skin was as white as milk, and her hair was fire-engine red. Despite her Latino and Middle Eastern ethnicity, she looked like a white woman, that had a ridiculously fat ass. Many said she had the uncanny resemblance to *Justina Valentine*, from Nick Cannon's hilarious '*Wild 'N Out*' comedy TV show. Kenzie was just taller and thicker than the red-headed mic monster.

Born and raised in Zion, Illinois, the fair-skinned stallion worked as a cashier and clerk at Wal-Mart. She was the loving mother of a 4-year-old little girl and did her best to be as responsible as she could be to support her daughter and herself. She did have help at some point, back when her daughter hadn't even been born.

Her baby daddy put a few dollars in her pocket every so often, more often than not, when she put his dick in her

128

mouth and let him fuck her in every hole, she had that he could put his dick in. Eventually, her bowel disease had gotten to him. Many times, she missed her chance to get to a bathroom on time when a flare-up happened, and it repulsed him. It brought him to the point that he had started beating on her, disrespecting her, and treating her like filth. Kenzie couldn't take it any longer and took the first step in rectifying her life, and with her first child being born, her daughter had become her priority.

Shrieking as a fart slipped out of her, Kenzie reached back with one hand and cupped her *48"* ass, pleading with her own body to hold on while she unlocked her car door. Dancing around as pressure in her bowels continued to build, she got her door open, jumped in, started the engine, then slamming it into drive, she mashed the gas and peeled out, nearly hitting a few people as she whipped it out the parking spot.

"Ooooo *shit, shit, shit, shit, shit, shit*! Come on! Fuck!" she panicked as she felt a turd threatening to slip out of her.

She floored it down the exit ramp to Route 173 then without even looking, she jumped out onto 173, cutting off a van as she whipped a hard left.

She sped her putt-putt to Kenosha Road and whipped a right turn at the light, then she put the pedal to the medal all the way to the entrance to the Horizon Village, where the one-bedroom apartment she lived in with her daughter was.

Kenzie raced down the asphalt drive, swerving around the circle, passing all the big apartment buildings until she got to the one, she and her daughter lived in.

She screeched to a stop in a spot that was closest to where her ground-level apartment's glass patio door was, hidden by the bushy 8-foot tall trees around it, and jumped out with her purse and keys, running like a maniac towards it.

"Ooooo no, no, no, no, no, no, *noooooo*!" she cried, feeling the turd pushing its way out of her rectum.

WHAM!

She was grabbed hard, and in the blink of an eye, a knee came flying into her gut with enough force to make her bowels explode.

The wind was knocked out of her. She fell to the ground, curling up into a fetal position. Curled up by her glass door, Kenzie cringed as she felt her panties filling up with hot mush and spreading around her rear end. A second later, she heard movement by her head. She looked up and saw her daughter's father there, with the look of pure evil in her eyes.

***

STACKS

He reached down and grabbed her and yanked her up off the ground. She screamed for help as he slammed her against the brick exterior wall of her apartment.

"Bitch, shut the fuck up!" he demanded, holding her against the wall by her throat, drawing his right hand back, balling his hand into a fist. "I'll break yo' muthafuckin' jaw right now! Scream again, bitch! Stanky-booty-ass slut!"

"D-Don-t-t-t! Please!" she begged, trying to pry his hand from around her neck.

"I *told* yo' stupid-ass I was gon' catch you!" he snapped.

Kenzie shitted on herself even more, and her bladder let go at the same time from the fear he instilled in her with his demonic glare.

"You's a *nasty-ass* hoe, joe!" Stacks spat.

Furiously, he snatched her away from the brick wall and as hard as he could, slammed her back into the glass window of her patio door.

The glass shattered. Kenzie screamed in pain as she was cut up from so many shards of glass hitting her skin.

Stacks looked at her, splayed out, bleeding, a big brown stain on the seat of her leggings.

"You's a waste of life! Fuck was I thinkin' gettin' yo' ass pregnant?!"

Filled with fury, Stacks ran up on her and started punching on her, trying to break her face. Covering her face with her hands, Kenzie screamed cried and begged for him to stop.

Stacks stopped beating her. Kenzie pulled her hands away from her face, only to discover that he had pulled out his cannon.

Stacks cocked it and pointed it at her face. "Talk that shit now, bitch! I dare you!" Stacks spat. "I should dome 'yo dumbass right now, joe! On the *Fin*!"

"Dontay! Please, baby! I'm-"

He cocked the pistol, stopping her from finishing her sentence. "Call me '*baby*' again, hoe! Say it again! I'ma shoot chu' in yo' mouth, bitch!"

Kenzie burst into tears, praying to God that the man she'd created life with, didn't take hers.

Just then, Stacks heard yelling from above. He looked up and saw the old woman that lived above Kenzie looking over her elevated deck railing.

"Hey! What are you doing? I'm calling the police!" the lady shouted.

"This shit ain't over, shitty-booty-bitch!" Stacks said to Kenzie. "I'ma shoot you in yo' ass crack if you don't pick the muthafuckin' phone up the next time I call! I don't give a *fuck* if you at work, on the toilet, sucking some dick, or sleep… if you don't answer the phone, yo ass dead, bitch!"

Stacks then ran out of the apartment and hopped into the black Chrysler 300C SRT-8 that he had bought just a few hours ago with some of the cash he and his crew swiped, dipping off and leaving his baby momma crying her eyes out.

***

JAVI

"Oh shit!" he shouted in panic, slamming on his brakes as a black Chrysler 300C shot through the west-bound red light at Route 41 and Route 173.

The rear wheels of his Large Car locked up. He started skidding sideways. Blasting the eardrum-piercing train horns his W900L had, he cursed out the driver of the STR-8 car as he came to within mere inches of t-boning it.

Luckily, the drive realized the mistake made and floored it, getting out of the way of the semi just in the nick of time.

"Dumbass!" he yelled out of the window as the car roared up 173, heading towards Antioch.

Letting off his brakes as he made it through the intersection, Javi heard his brother call to him through the CB radio.

"Yo, bro! You aight?!" Xavier asked.

Xavier, Evelyn, and ChaCha were behind him, having trailed him up from Romeoville.

Javi reached for his CB mike and unhooked it. "Fuckin' clown must have a death wish, man! Who does that shit?!"

ChaCha's voice came through the radio. "Dumbass people need to stay off the road, yo. On the real, son."

"Next muhfucka that does that shit, I'ma flatten 'em! On my *momma*!" Javi swore, as he came up on the D.O.T weight station for southbound truck traffic only.

Exiting the highway, Javi, Xavier, and Evelyn parted ways from ChaCha. They went left on Russell Road while she went right to get to where her own PJ&D Transport yard was, up on Kilbourne Road.

"Holla," they all heard her say over the radio.

Turning onto Frontage Road, Javi saw two of his sister's lady trucks pulling out of the yard.

In the shiny metallic green Peterbilt 388, built to transport ten vehicles was Payton. In the identical red and black 2-tone Peterbilt behind her was Olivia.

The ladies tooted their air horns as they passed Javi, Xavier, and their boss.

"Glad to see y'all made it back," Javi heard Payton say. "See y'all tomorrow."

Javi saw through the fence that three bays of his garage were open, and the heavy-haul trucks driven by the guys in his brother's *Specialized Freight* crew, inside getting serviced.

Xavier's good friend Thurgood was filling up the engine oil reservoir of his maroon-colored 2014 Peterbilt 389, which was coupled up with a heavy-duty Low-boy trailer.

In the other two bays, Xavier's own heavy hauler was getting its oil changed. Besides the W900L he was in, he had another W9 that was heavy-spec'd and chromed out so much that it could enter custom truck *and* car shows and win.

In the bay next to where Xavier's heavy-haul Large Car was, the red Kenworth T800, driven by his homeboy Pete.

Pete and Thurgood took great care of their expensive trucks and trailers, and often Xavier's, just to help him out whenever he wasn't around to do it himself.

The remaining five of Evelyn's auto-transport trucks were parked in a row. Like the two that had just left the yard, they could carry up to ten vehicles, depending on the size. Seven could fit on the trailer, and three more on the steel frame that was built onto the tractor.

Evelyn also had a couple of spare rigs in her fleet, in case of break downs...or reckless drivers, like Nena, whose broken down Peterbilt was still sitting in the garage, not making a dime.

For her and her girlfriend, Evelyn had two luxurious and ridiculously expensive 53'-long enclosed 2010 Kentucky 6-car transport trailers. They were like NASCAR trailers. Each had run Javi $350,000, not including the custom paint jobs that they now sported, to match Evelyn's big Volvo 780, and her girlfriend's Kenworth T660. Evelyn and Gloria used the two-luxury car-carriers to transport some of the most expensive vehicles in the world, and just off that, they checked a stupid bag every week.

All nine of Javi's drivers were there in the yard. Most of them had their women and kids with them. Their trucks and trailers were all parked in their designated spots, shining from being washed and detailed before being parked.

There was O-Boy, a rowdy light-skinned guy from down Chicago's south side. He was a Black Disciple, from the well-known O-Block neighborhood that was represented proudly by Chicago's famous OTF mob. O-Boy was joined by his girl Jeannette, and their twin 6-year-old daughters Myra and Kyra.

Tank, the massive Samoan beast was with his Hawaiian girlfriend Heaven.

Bull, a big husky dark-skinned man from, the west side of Chicago, was with his wife Chante.

JB, the only one of the crew from up West Allis in Wisconsin, was there with *two* of his sexy Mexican women, Claudia and Maribel. EZ Money, Cadillac, Sergio, Pistols, and Black were all with their women as well; Cadillac and his girl Leatha's children, Teresa and Terrance, had tagged along with them. Black and his woman's daughter Emma, well-known for wanting to be a truck driver when she was old enough, was enjoying a day with her big trucker father, getting a little education from his teachings.

They all turned and started shouting and cheering as Javi turned into the yard ahead of his brother and sister. Feeling the love like *Money Making Mitch* when the young fresh and fly dope boy hit the block in the clean red drop-top Beemer with *Ace Boogie*, when he got out of jail, Javi started revving his engine up and tooting his train horns, showing off a little bit. The kids shouted and cheered even louder. He and the rest of the Dedicated crew had them *all* wanting to be truckers when they grew up.

***

Javi backed his Large Car up to the garage bay door for his indoor-parking spot and parked, putting his E-Log onto *Off-Duty*, then cut his engine off. He got out of the cab and was immediately greeted by so many '*HAPPY BIRTHDAY!*' shout-outs from the kids and the crew. The children were one of his favorite parts of being involved with his drivers. He couldn't wait to have a few little ones of his own.

"Yo, yo, yo! Check it out, young ones!" Javi said to the shorties. "Who's tryna' make some money?" he asked them.

"Meeee!" they all hollered together, jumping up and down excitedly.

With their parents, Xavier, and Evelyn gathered around, Javi started hitting them with some CDL knowledge questions, testing to see who still wanted to drive trucks when they got older.

"Okay! Who can tell meee," He paused, for dramatic effect, "what the tire tread depth *needs* to be for... front tires?"

"4/32 of an inch!" shouted O-Boy's daughter Myra.

"Yes!" Javi dug in his pocket and pulled out the wad of cash he'd taken out of the bank he had made a stop at on the way from Joliet, knowing the kids were there, and could continue to motivate them all to keep up the good work by putting some money in their hands.

He pulled out a $100 and gave it to Myra. She jumped up and down, ecstatic with joy, then she ran to where her sister, mother, and father were standing. The three congratulated her emphatically.

"Next one!" Javi said, holding another honcho out. "What is *the* most important reason for doin' a pre-trip inspection?"

"Safety!" shouted Cadillac's son Terrance.

"Correct!" Javi gave Terrance the hundred-dollar bill. Terrance went bananas with excitement, waving his years' worth of bubble gum money around like it was the golden ticket to Willy Wonka's chocolate factory. "Okay! Let's make this one a *little* harder!" Javi held up two $100s now, smiling at the youngsters with anticipation.

They all stood poised and ready to answer whatever he threw at them. Even their parents were geeked to see what question Javi was going to hit them with.

"Who can tell me how many times the shifter for an 18-speed transmission actually moves?" Javi asked, remembering all the times that he'd heard people say they couldn't drive a truck because they didn't want to be shifting eighteen gears all the time.

Black's daughter Emma caught this one.

"Nine times, Javi!" she shouted enthusiastically, then she broke it down, knowing Javi would ask her to explain. "An 18-speed has five gears in the low-range, and four in the high-range, but each one has a *Low* and a *High*! That makes each of them basically two gears in one!"

"And nine times two is?"

"Eighteen!" they all shouted at once.

Javi congratulated all of them and handed Emma her deuce, then he asked more questions until he was out of money, and the kids had split $1,500 dollars.

Evelyn walked up to her big brother and hugged him. "You're gonna make a great father one day, bro," she told him, smooching him on his cheek. "As long as you stop fuckin' cheatin' on Michelle with that nasty-mouth traga leche."

"No se que hablas," Javi capped.

"Yes, you do know what the fuck I'm talkin' 'bout, but it's all good. Keep playin', and Michelle gon' turn that thot-ass bitch into Alpo." She kissed his face again. "I still love you, though, you old ass man."

"I love you, too, sis," Javi replied with a chuckle, then added, "and shut up."

His sister had a point. The more he thought about how he had been being so grimy, cheating on the woman that had his heart, the more he felt like scum. He hated feeling like that. He knew there was only one way to feel pure.

At that moment, Javi decided that he was not ever fucking around with Angela again, not matter what.

Chapter 14
JAVI

Javi manually drained all the air out of his Kenworth's air tank, expelling all compressor oil and water, so that neither would potentially freeze in his air lines and reduce the braking power he had when he set back out.

While air released, he responded to a text from his woman. Tank walked up just then and told him about one of the Rojas-Gomez cartel stash houses getting hit up, and everyone inside kicking it there were murdered.

"Damn!" Javi said, shaking his head. "Fuck Victor Gomez, but I don't like hearin' innocent women bein' killed because of clown-ass dudes. Whoever did that, they finna check a big stupid meat roll off what they came up on, but the heat finna be unbearable for them when dude's bitchass find out who they are, and… he *will*."

"I'm happy for them, Javi," Tank admitted. "Fuck Victor Gomez. Anything bad that happens to him, I'm geeked to hear it."

Javi knew the giant despised Victor, maybe even more than he did. Tank and O-Boy had been in their trucks when Victor Gomez had them shot up. Truth be told, Tank wasn't really tripping about having been in it when it got lit up. He was more pissed that it had happened when he had his girlfriend with him.

"Dude sent more hitters at us, too," Javi informed him. "For some reason, muhfuckas think we ain't ready at all times to get it crackin', wherever we stand."

Tank grew furious at that news. He hadn't heard about the ambush.

"Man, *fuck* this shit, Javi! Yo let's just go to *every* Fast Lane terminal and blow *'erybody* the fuck down! Make him come to us, then I'ma buss' his muhfuckin' head open!"

Javi really wanted to, but he shook his head. "We can't, big homie. Not yet. ChaCha got on our ass about hitting his Antioch yard last week. We'll get him, though, bro. He's likely expectin' us to strike back right now, like we some dummies; we finna make him sweat, wonder when are we comin'. I wanna' make him lose sleep, thinkin' one day, one of us gon' be in his bedroom, pointin' a banger at his face. If we stay one step ahead of dude, then *we* are winnin', you dig?"

At that, Tank nodded his head in understanding. "I dig, bro. Say the word and I'm ready to ride. Happy birthday again, too, homie."

"Grassy-ass, Tank roll," Javi replied graciously, dapping the big man up. "Now go enjoy the day with your lady. I need to get home, but I'll be back a little later," he said, then with all the air out of his tank, he closed the valve back and went to hop into his Wraith, throwing up the deuces at everyone as he rolled out.

***

STACKS

"On *'erythang*, lord, I almost just *died!*" Stacks exclaimed, heart still beating fast as he sat parked in his STR-8 300C. "A truck almost took me clean out, joe!"

"Fuck you runnin' red lights for, lord? You already hot from beatin' yo' baby momma up 'n shit!" Rambo fired back at him. "*And*, 12 lookin' fo' us for bussin' that thang, joe! Yo ass tweakin' hard, man!"

Stacks waved his mans off. "Bruh, the boys don't have no clue about suspects. It's all over the news; you ain't been seein' WGN? They think it was some goof-ass white boys. Chill out with that 'noid shit, lord."

He heard Rambo groan with frustration. "Man, just be cool, bruh. We don't need no extra heat. Let's get this money and be Ghosts like we supposed to be."

"You right, joe. I'm gone from it," Stacks told his guy.

"We'll see," Rambo replied wearily. "But, aye, joe. Maan, somethin' is up with yo' lil' bitch's brother. On the 5, his ass weird as fuck. He stay starin' at me, like a bitch that wanna fuck."

Stacks busted out laughing. "*Wooooooow*! Aye, lord! Mikey wants the *D*, joe, and I don't mean *DOPE*!"

"On the Fin, stop playin' with me, Stacks! On Ghost, that shit is not funny! I'll knock his lil' dome off if I find out he a homo!"

"He tryna knock 'yo dome off, joe!" Stacks continued, still laughing.

Rambo got pissed off and ended the call.

Wiping the tears from his eyes from laughing so hard, Stacks sat back in his chair, waiting for his customer to pull up and cop what he had ordered.

Sitting at a gas station at the corner of Route 45 and Route 173 in Antioch, Stacks was directly across from a huge truck company that had suffered serious fire damage. He saw there was yellow police line around the whole property, and a couple of crime scene investigator vans. Stacks wondered what the heck had happened, because it looked like someone pissed another some off, *really* bad.

Ten minutes later, the silver BMW 535i entered the gas station and pulled in next to Stacks. The driver, a white guy that looked like a surfer from California, walked over nonchalantly, and hopped into the front seat of Stacks car.

"What 'oun, Dave?" Stacks said to the guy, dapping him up.

"What's up, Stacks? Good lookin' out on meetin' up with me, dog," Dave said, as he pulled out three $5,000 wads of cash from the pockets of his khaki cargo shorts. "Nobody has dope as good as yours, man. It's so dry, so I'm about get frickin' *narly* rich, dude!"

"A quarter of a brick of dope ain't gon' make you narly anything, joe," Stacks told him, counting the cash before he handed the man anything, "but it *is* a start."

Counting five grand, Stacks got the quarter brick from under his hoodie and gave it to Dave. They shook hands and the guy got out, hopping back into his Beemer and pulling off.

Stacks exited the gas station and headed south on 45, making his way towards Round Lake. As he cruised, nodding his head to Lil' Durk, Magali called him.

"Bae, I'm down in the hood and, jeeeoooo! This shit is movin'!" she exclaimed, super geeked.

"Good. Gon' 'n get that shit off then come bring daddy that change, then I need some of that fi' ass head and pussy."

"Mmmmmm, I love it when you talk to me like that, papi. I'll be back up asap."

"Yup. Aye? Is yo' lil brother gay?" Stacks asked, as the conversation between him and Rambo popped into his head.

"Uh... huh?"

"Fuck you mean 'huh?' Bitch, is you deaf?"

"My bad. Someone was callin' me, baby. What did you ask?"

"Is Mikey gay?"

"No."

"Rambo think he is; he said Mikey be eyin' him like a bitch do who she tryna fuck."

Magali busted out laughing. "No, baby, my little brother ain't no puñal. He's just... very observant. He did time before, and it's kind of stuck with him."

"I hope for *his* sake that you right. Lord'll murk his ass if shorty really *do* get down like that."

"Stacks, if yo' guy touches my brother, I'ma pop the *fuck* outta his bitchass, joe. That's *on* my momma!"

Stacks started laughing. "Get at me, lil' mama," he told her, then ended the call.

Cruising along behind a steady flow of southbound traffic, doing the speed limit, Stacks drove right to avoid the eyes of the Lake County Sheriffs that loved posting along 45. He heard Rambo's words in his head, warning him to be cool, so he made it a point to act like a leader, instead of a clown.

***

JAVI

Heading east down Wadsworth Road from Route 41, Javi made his way towards Beach Park, where he and his woman lived. He cruised at the speed limit, nodding his head to Lil' Durk, happy to be home and adding another one to the books.

Passing through the Wadsworth and Lewis Ave intersection, he continued along the hilly and constantly curving two-way valley road, passing small homes that sat on grassy hills, tucked slightly back from the street.

Minutes later, as he passed a line of tall bushy trees on his left that allowed nobody to see beyond them, Javi came to a near hidden stone-paved driveway. He came to a stop and after the on-coming traffic passed, he turned in and rolled onwards onto his one -and-a-half-acre residential property.

To his right was a stall retaining wall made of stone, keeping the dirt covered hill on the south side of his property from spilling onto the driveway, ran all the way up to the mansion that sat at the top of the upward inclining driveway.

To the left, down a hill was a long creek that flowed down from where the house was. Beyond it, a jungle of a yard, full of trees, bushes, and all sorts of other foliage. It was like he had his own wilderness.

Three minutes later, the luxurious 10,250-square-foot log-cabin-style mansion appeared at the end of the driveway. With it, a 10-car garage that was built to replicate the mansion.

Javi's house looked like that of a luxury cabin out in the snowy mountains of Aspen, Colorado, one where after being out all day, getting it in, true peace and tranquility was brought by such a grand abode.

The mansion was 2-stories high, with big windows in front, a big porch with wooden pillars holding up an awning roof. Inside, the entire main floor was styled in a an open-concept design, all connected to a massive Great Room that had high ceilings with exposed wood beams, and a glass retracting door to the spacious backyard.

Six big bedrooms, not including the humongous master bed and bathroom; five full bathrooms, a big chef's-style kitchen fitted with stainless Italian-brand appliances, marble floors and granite counter tops.

Javi and his woman had the best of the best included into their home's build. They truly lived in luxury, whenever they were out, and whenever they were in.

Parking his Wraith at the front porch, Javi hopped out with his bag and went up the porch steps to the custom-made glass and gold framed French door. At the side of it, he put his watch to the scanner there. Inside the vintage Cartier on his wrist, he'd had a special sensor added in that was synchronized with the touch and codeless house security system. Should anyone without a sensor on their person step onto their porch, the hidden .30 caliber torrent guns that were programed to descend from the exterior ceiling would blow them to pieces in seconds.

The security system disarmed, and the doors unlocked. Javi entered the cool fresh smelling mansion with a smile.

"*Maaan*, I never felt so happy to be home," he said to himself, heading through the deluxe Great Room to the kitchen.

He went right to the big stainless Sub-Zero French-door refrigerator and got a cold Presidente out, popping the top and taking a healthy gulp of the ice cold and crisp Dominican beer.

Heading towards the stairs to get up to his bedroom, Javi took another gulp, savoring taste, when he saw Diamond and Demon, both sitting side by side at the top of the stairs, looking down at him.

"What the hell?" Javi made his way up the stairs and came to a stop when he got to his big Cane Corsos. "I could've *sworn* Michelle took y'all with her," he said, patting both on their heads.

Javi bought the two Sicilian Mastiffs straight from a breeder in Sicily, when they were pups. Their pedigree dating back to the 1800s, making their value in the six-digit range. The training he had invested in them came from being taught by the close friend of his big cousin Macho, whom had been in the dog breeding and training game since he was a youngster.

Demon stood 24" tall at his shoulders, weighed 110 pounds, had a massive head, with a bite force that was as powerful as a Spotted Hyena, the one animal in the world with the *strongest* bite force ever recorded for a carnivorous animal.

Diamond was his female equivalent. She was 10 pounds lighter, 2" shorter, and her head was smaller, but her bite force was damn near as powerful as her mate's. They both could bite through human bone, with ease.

Javi kissed Diamond's nose as her tail wagged excitedly for his return. Demon licked his face, tail wagging happily as well. A second later, Javi heard Remy Ma's *Feels So Good* featuring Ne-Yo playing from his bedroom.

His jaw dropped. A gasp escaped him. He looked at the two monsters. Demon barked, his ears perking up straight.

"No way… she can't be back already," he said to himself, then he quick-stepped to the bedroom, entering to see the lights on, but dimmed.

The big master was so exclusive that most A-List celebrities would grow envious of the design. Amongst everything that made it the bedroom of a filthy rich man and woman, the wall of floor-to-ceiling windows could turn opaque at the touch of a button on a remote.

Oh snap….daaaaaaaaaaayuuuuuuuuuum! Javi thought to himself, when he saw her there, leaning against their huge Maree luxury bed, ordered straight out of a DuPont Registry magazine.

There she was, waiting for him, in the sexiest lingerie ever. Javi's amazingly beautiful dominicana had her hair loose and wet. Smokey eyelids and hot red lipstick gave her the look of a sexy vixen that was so hot and ready for a few rounds. She had on a red lace bra with red fishnet thigh-high stockings clipped onto a red lace garter belt, but with *no* panties at all. Red 6" stilettos were on her feet, giving her 5'5" frame a little more height.

Javi's dick got hard as a steel pipe immediately. He nearly floated over to her, not even realizing he was moving until he was right in front of her.

"¡*Diablos*, bebe!" he exclaimed, dumbfounded by how bad his chick was. "¡Tu 'ta *buena!* Holy shit!"

Michelle smirked at him so seductively that Javi could've busted a nut just off that.

"Happy birthday, mi sexy tiguere," she said to him, then she reached out to undo his pants, and free his hardness. "Allow me to give you the first of 25 blowjobs that I plan to give you today."

Then she sank down to her knees, pulling his pants and boxer briefs with her, to the floor.

Javi watched in glee as she planted a kiss on the tip of his dick with her sexy red lips, the stick her tongue out and swirl it around it, running it down the side of his shaft, to the base, then to his balls.

"Oooohhhh shhhhhhhit!" he cursed, as she sucked his balls into her mouth and massaged them. "Whoa, whoa, whoa, whoa, whoooaaa! ¡Coño, mamita!"

She released his balls after pleasuring them for a few minutes, then she took his dick into her mouth, deep throating him like a pro. She sucked and gagged on it, let it out and spit on it, then inhaled his hard cock back into her mouth and went crazy on him.

Javi groaned and cursed repeatedly until he could no longer take it. He needed to feel her warm wet pussy that *always* crippled him when he busted a nut.

"¡Que se joda, baby! I know it's *my* birthday, but *I* got a present for *you*," he said, taking his dick out of her mouth, pulling her up from the floor, and tossing her on the bed.

Michelle scooted to the middle of the bed, knees bent up, opening wide for him, licking her lips as he stripped completely naked.

"Ay, papi, me gusta lo que veo," she purred as her pussy got even wetter from the sight of his chiseled and tattooed body.

She put two fingers at her slit and played with her kitty cat for him. Javi hopped on the bed, ready to do that for her. He dove his face between her legs and went in on her, tasting her goodness, once he'd parted her swollen pussy lips. Michelle hissed with bliss, feeling him sucking her clit, swirling his tongue around it at the same time.

"¡Aayy! Javi! Ooooo, Dios mio! ¡Asi, papi! Just like that!" she told him, reaching her hands down and running them over his braided head.

"This pussy taste so good, baby," he hummed to her, pulling his face up for a second to express how much he loved her flavor.

"It's the freshest pussy on earth! Now shut it up and eat it up!"

He went back in for more and kept it up until her body arched all the way up off the bed and started trembling. She cursed as he brought her closer.

"Oooooo, I'm gonna cum, papi! ¡Me voy a venir!" she announced a minute later.

Adding two fingers inside of her to make her crave penetration, Javi ate her and finger-fucked her at the same time. He kept it going until she exploded, squirting all in his face, soaking it like he had submerged it in a sink full of water.

"*Shit!*" she cursed out at the tops of her lungs from how hard he had just made her climax.

"I hope you don't think it's over, punk, 'cause I'ma 'bout to go nuts on yo' ass, amor," he told her, and before she could even respond, Javi had flipped her over onto her stomach and was pulling her hips upwards.

Ass down, face up he got her. Michelle bit her bottom lip and moaned as he put his face in between her cheeks. His lips kissed her asshole, then he stuck his tongue out and licked around it, then he stuck it in her ass, snaking it around inside of her chute.

Michelle squealed and shrieked from the super dirty freaky nasty sensation. She loved how Javi went so hard to please her. There were no doors with him. He did whatever it took to make her happy. Sexually, physically, mentally, spiritually, and emotionally, Javi treated her like the queen she was to him, and she could never get enough of it.

She buried her face in the bed as he continued his oral-ass-assault. He lifted his face up a minute later, spit a wad onto her brown eye and gripped his throbbing cock in his hand.

147

Michelle reached her hands back and held her cheeks open for him. She felt the tip of his bulbous dick inch into her chute, slowly and gently easing in, further and further. She felt the stinging pain but welcomed it. He went even further in, then stopped to check on her.

"You okay, baby?" he asked her.

"Yeeesss! Fuck me, Javi!" she told him.

Javi obliged her and stroked her, fucking her asshole and making her toes curl up. She climaxed again in less than five minutes while he was smacking on her ass and pulling her hair.

Javi kept on going until he felt his own nut ready to pop off. He groaned gutturally, cursing up a storm as he felt it rise.

Michelle could feel his cock spasming inside of her tract. She reached back, hurried to pull him out, then forcing him off the bed, onto his feet, she fell back down to her knees before him and let him put it back into her mouth.

Javi fucked her face until he exploded. He came so hard that his knees almost gave out.

"Ooooo fuuuucckk! ¡Diablos!" he howled as he emptied the clip down her throat.

Michelle swallowed every drop like his jizz was the tastiest thing on earth. With a smile on her face, she grabbed his cock and kissed the tip of it before it got soft.

"Holy shit… that was crazy," Javi said to her.

Michelle started laughing. "I hope you don't think it's over, *punk*, 'cause I'ma 'bout to go nuts on *yo'* ass," she told him, throwing his words back at him.

"Can I get some water first?" he asked her.

"Nope! Let's go!" she demanded, then pushed him back onto the bed and jumped on him.

Michelle got two more nuts out of her birthday man, and got five more off herself, before they were completely spent of energy. Laying together, Michelle's leg over his, his arms around her, her head on his chest, their bodies sweaty and hot, they both gazed into each other's eyes.

"I love you so much, Javier," she told him, feeling like she was the queen of his world.

"I love you even more, Michelle," he replied, adoring the beautiful dominicana so much that he despised himself for even thinking about piping another chick down, much less doing it.

"Let's take a nap. When we wake up, I need to do your hair, and we need to get ready."

"Ready? For what?" Javi asked her, with a puzzled look.

She started grinning. "We're going to a nice little get-together with your family, bae. It's your b-day."

"Awww, come oooon, Michelle. Can't we just stay home and fuck?"

She laughed at him. "Tomorrow we can, but tonight, I am taking my man to kick back with those that love him dearly. So, close your eyes with me, and when we wake up, up and at it."

He groaned. "Okay."

Chapter 15
XAVIER

Pamela squealed in delight when Xavier stuck his middle finger in her asshole as she bounced up and down on his dick in the spacious 72" mid-roof aerodyne-style sleeper berth that was in the back of the cab of his W900L. The Venezuelan beauty *loved* that freaky-ass shit. Between him and watching Porn Hub, she considered herself perfectly matched for his sex-game.

The curtains that separated the cab and the sleeper were closed, giving them privacy while so many people, and children, were in the yard. T-Pain's *Blow Ya Mind* played, bumping from the custom Rockford Fosgate sound-system wired in his rig.

Pamela's succulent 32D cups bounced in Xavier's face as she went wild on his dick. He laid back so she could go even crazier on him.

The 28-year-old was another one of Xavier's breezies. Recently a graduate of medical school, she was surely going places. Brains and beauty were Xavier's steelo.

Pamela was 5'3" tall. Her skin was the color of honey. Her petite body was virtually flawless, and her long silky sandy-brown hair reached down to her 38" ass. She had a little slim face that was framed by black Gucci frames, a diamond stud in her right nostril, and she had a diamond choker chain around her neck. She had a few tattoos that added such sex appeal to her exotic nerdiness.

"Fuck!" she cried out as she felt herself ready to cum.

She threw her head back and exploded all over him seconds later.

Xavier quickly put her onto her back, climbed on top, and grabbing her right leg, hooking his arm under it, he slid back into her and power-fucked her until she came again.

She took over afterwards, getting him back onto his back. She took his thick 10" cock into her mouth and sucked him until he busted his nut. Sucking it all out of him, Pamela spit his cum out onto his gut and like a thirsty kitty, she slurped it all back up, giggling as she finished him off.

"Mmmmm, tastes so good, baby," she purred to him, licking her lips.

"Yo' ass a true freak, baby. Straight up," he told her.

"So? Ain't nothing wrong with making it nasty for my man," she replied. "I'm a bad bitch so it's only right for me to be a freak."

Xavier chuckled, but he liked her logic, though he didn't like when she called him her man. She knew what it was between them. Fucking and dating, not a relationship. But she chose to ignore that, hoping that one day he would just claim her.

"So, can we kick it tonight, baby?" she asked, climbing up and lying next to him, resting her arm on his muscular chest and stroking his chin with a finger. "I been wanting to spend the night with you since I graduated med school."

"No promises, mamita, but I will try. It's my brother's b-day, so you already know I gots to kick it with him."

"Ooooo! Can I come, too?" she asked with eyes lit up with excitement.

He thought about it. Nena was going to be there and would most definitely try to fight— no, *kill* Pamela. And he still needed to go see Keisha.

"I'ma see what's up, aight? I need to make a couple move right now, though. Where you gon' be later on?" he asked, as he sat up to grab his clothes.

"At home, probably playing with my pussy while I picture you all up in it, all night long."

"Okay, then." He chuckled. "Get dressed. We'll link up later, bonita."

***

EVELYN

"Fucking slut-bucket-ass bitch!" Evelyn growled to herself as she watched the scantily clad Venezolana get out of her middle brother's truck, reaching under her skirt to pull her re-adjust her thong.

"Don't start that shit, Eve."

Forgetting that she was on the phone with her girlfriend, Evelyn jumped when she heard Gloria's voice came out of the speakers of her BMW.

"Your brother is a very handsome man, so of course he's gonna have a lot of hoes."

"Bitch! Ain't nobody ask you! Mind yo business, joe! Fuck wrong wit' chu' you!"

"Come home 'n talk that shit, *biiitch*! I'll beat cho' ass and make Oinky pee in yo' face, hoe!"

Evelyn busted out laughing at her girlfriend. "Leave my piggy up outta it, mamahuevo," she said, as she watched her brother's bitch head over to her gleaming red Audi A4, and Xavier hop into his Range Rover. "I'm on the way, though. I need some sleep before we head down to the city for the bash."

***

STACKS

Stacks parked his STR-8 300C in the parking lot of a Big Lots, out in Round Lake, right off Rollins and Cedar Lake

Road. While he waited for the next customer to pull up, he rolled up a blunt of *Purple Haze* and sparked it up.

Puffing on his loud pack, he started feeling the effects of the strong marijuana after two tokes. He had the windows up, hot boxing the whip, getting angry from having to wait.

Halfway through the blunt, the dark blue Escalade he was expecting pulled into the lot. He watched it roll towards him, then turning into the lane he was in, made another turn into the spot next to him then parked.

Stacks waited as Reggie got out of the Caddy truck and pimp-walked like a clown around the rear to hop into his Chrysler.

"What 'oun, lord?" Reggie said, as he reached a fist out to Stacks to dap him up.

Stacks looked at the dark-skinned man's fist then, looking at him, he blew Purp Smoke in Reggie's face.

"I been smokin' on this loud fo' about 20 minutes now, dirty as hell *in* Round Lake. You was 'supposed to be here *20 minutes* ago. What the fuck makes you think I'ma dap yo' clown-ass up right now?"

Reggie retracted his fist. "My fault, joe. I was tryna get the last of my chop together from the brothas'. On my crown, my bad, joe."

Stacks shook his head.

A Black man claimin' to be a Latin King... what's next? White Black Stones and white Black Disciples? he thought to himself.

"Where my money at, *King?*" Stacks asked, very sarcastically.

Reggie pulled out a brown paper bag from the front pocket of his hoodie and handed it to Stacks. As Stacks opened it up, Reggie's heart started beating a mile a minute. He didn't have all the money for the brick of coke he was there to cop, and he knew that Stacks was a ticking time bomb.

Stacks frowned when he counted only $10,000 in the bag. "You *must* be out cho' rabbit-ass mind to waste my time with this bullshit. You late, then you get in my whip and only got *half* of the money?!"

He looked over at Reggie and saw how scared he was.

"Lord, on *360*, I swear, my fault. I'll give you an extra ten-gees if you hit me with this brick, joe," Reggie tried to bargain. "One of my brothas got caught up with the other half."

"That ain't my problem! Man, get the fuck out my car!" Stacks demanded.

"Aight, aight, aight! My bad, lord!" Reggie said, reaching over for the money.

"Naw, joe. This is my money now, famo," Stacks told him.

Reggie looked gobsmacked. "Wh-what? What 'chu mean, joe?"

"Muhfuckas *love* runnin' off of on the plug; this is *me*, the plug, runnin' off on *yo'* bitchass! Get the fuck out my shit, bitch!" Stacks yelled, pulling his banger from his waistline and putting it to Reggie's temple.

"L-L-Lord! C-come on, j-j-joe!" Reggie pleaded. "That's Nation money!"

"I do not give a fuck about yo' nation. You a Black man reppin' a Latin mob. You's a clown. Get out or get popped."

"Stacks! Please, man!"

"One! Two! Thr-"

"Okay, okay, okay!" Reggie yelled, and was out of the Chrysler in seconds, hopping into his Escalade and tearing out of the lot like a whole neighborhood of Latin Folks were on his ass.

Stacks busted out laughing at the coward. He put his whip into drive and pulled off before someone called the cops to report the altercation.

He called Rambo as he made a left turn onto Rollins to head back towards Gurnee.

"What 'oun, joe?" Rambo answered.

"Aye, lord! On Ghost! These Lake County muhfuckas are some straight up hoes!"

"What happened?"

Stacks told his guy what he had just did.

"Fam, you know them Kings be on that wild shit, joe. Why is you robbin' them?" Rambo asked, knowing who Reggie was associated with.

"Man don't nobody give a fuck about the Lake County gangbangers. The way I see it, it's the mobsters from the Land that are the real 'monstas. The Kings from Crown Town, 26 & California, and Humboldt Park, muhfuckas'll think twice 'bout pullin' it with them, but theses Outta-Town-ass clowns sweet like butter popcorn. Fuck *Snake* County, joe."

Rambo was silent for a minute.

"Aye, man. Lemme' find out you getting' soft on me from bein' out here too long?" Stacks said, as he cruised along a small highway like section.

"Never."

"Aight. You knew what I was on when I told you I was tryna come out here. We finna buss' these licks, then shoot back home when we got some *M*s and put the hood on."

"I hear you, bruh. His me up later, though. I'm with my baby momma."

"Yo cuddy-buddy-ass," Stacks teased, then ended the call.

***

XAVIER

Later That Evening

Xavier left out of Keisha's one-bedroom apartment, out in the Horizon Village of Zion, drained of energy and cum. She'd milked him for everything. He was surprised he could even walk.

As he exited through the main access hallway, another apartment door opened up and out stepped the thickest white girl he had ever seen.

GODDAAAAMN! he thought to himself, seeing so much ass in tight purple leggings.

She was tall, curvy, with fire-engine red hair, and she was *gorgeous!*

She look just like that white chick from Nick Cannon's TV show with the red hair, he thought again, looking at the girl's face.

The voluptuous red head had three duffel bags and a book bag that had butterflies and ponies on it. It was at that moment that Xavier noticed that her hands and arms were covered with bandages. He looked up at her face again, and saw a cut in her cheek, and above her left eyebrow.

Immediately, his heart dropped when he realized something very bad had happened to this beautiful woman.

The girl took a step away from the door and looked up. She saw him and gasped, then seemed to freeze where she stood.

"Hey?" he called to her. "You okay, ma?"

The girl didn't reply. She looked down at her Nikes.

"Excuse me, miss," Xavier said, taking a step towards her.

She gasped and took a step back, dropping her bags and blocking her face.

"Please! Don't hit me!" she begged, backing up against the wall.

"Whoa, whoa… hit you? Naw, ma. I'm a man. I don't hit women. Bitches do that shit."

She looked at him, then her bags, as if contemplating grabbing them and making a run for it.

"Yo boyfriend do this to you?" he asked her.

She didn't answer. She just continued looking down, obviously petrified of something.

"My name is Xavier," he then said. "Xavier Valdez. I am not gonna' hurt you, ma. I'd just like to know if you need some help?"

She stayed quiet for a minute longer, then, her eyes rolled up, looking so red and puffy.

"Y-You can't help me," she stammered. "Nobody can."

"If you let me, I bet you I could. I'm pretty well-liked, and I do not honor humans that call themselves men but think it's okay to lay their hands on women," he told her. "I swear to you, ma. I can help you. What's yo' name?"

She hesitated but then told him.

"K-Kenzie… Cardoza."

"Cardoza? You're Latina?" he asked her, with sudden interest.

"Half, Cuban and Armenian."

Damn! No wonder why she's so fuckin' beautiful! Xavier thought.

"Oh, okay. I can't 'een lie, ma. I thought you was a *guera*," he told her.

She wasn't fluent in Spanish, but she knew enough. Having been called a *guera* or a *gringa* most of her life, she knew all too well what he was saying he thought she was.

"I'm Dominican," Xavier told her then, which unbeknownst to her, he had just confirmed her wonders of what he might be, due to the way he pronounced the word by rolling the 'R' perfectly. "And if you don't mind me sayin' this, Kenzie Cardoza, you are an *extremely* beautiful woman."

His words managed to make her smile.

"Thank you, Xavier."

He nodded. "No problem. Look." He took a deep breath and went for it. "It's really hurtin' me right now to see such a beautiful woman lookin' as terrified as you. I seriously won't be able to sleep tonight if I just let you go, without helpin' you, somehow, some way. Please? Can I lend you a hand?"

"I... I don't know how you can. My...my daughter's father, he's crazy. I have to get us out of town before he kills us."

Hearing that he was right about some guy having did the girl so bad sparked a fire in Xavier's chest. Even worse, her child's father.

"Yo' baby daddy did that to you?"

She nodded.

"Where's your daughter at?"

"She's at my momma house. I have to go get her, then we're gonna go."

Xavier felt that she was warming up to him a little, which told her she wasn't afraid of him, but of her situation.

"You gon' let a square run you off, though, ma?". he asked.

"I can't stay, Xavier! Stacks will freakin' kill me! He threw me through my patio window and he made me... he beat me! Then he pulled a gun on me and pointed it at my face!"

"Then come with *me* then, Kenzie," he said, before he even realized it.

Kenzie looked at him, her eyes filled with surprise. "Wh-what?"

Xavier took a step towards her. "I know you and I don't know each other for squat, but I can protect you and your little girl."

"But... my baby daddy-"

"Is a *peon*," Xavier said, cutting her off. He took out his wallet that was filled with big faces and credit and debit cards, along with a *Black card*, fishing out his license. He handed it to her. "This is my personal information; my name, address, all that. I want you to trust me and come with me. We can go get your daughter, then y'all can come to my crib. I literally live on the opposite side of 173, right around the corner from here, as you can see on my license. Or, we can go wherever you want to go. Even to another country. That's word."

Kenzie had no actual clue who the man in front of her was, but what she did know, was that he gave her a feeling of comfort, and security. She looked into his eyes and saw honesty, truth, sincerity. The way he spoke was with mad passion. And, as big and muscular as he was, if he had really wanted to hurt her, he looked like he could snap her in half without much effort.

"O-okay. But I just don't want to involve you in my drama, Xavier," Kenzie told him. "I swear, my baby daddy is a real live gangster."

"And I'm a man, Kenzie," Xavier told her, reaching down to grab her bags for her, then looked into her eyes and added, "and a man is *always* stronger, tougher, and braver than any goon or gangster."

Chapter 16
VICTOR

Pushing his restored 1993 Land Rover Defender south on Lewis Avenue, the Corvette engine under the hood growled out of the sporty exhaust, creating the most spine-tingling sound. Victor rolled through the busy shopping area in Waukegan, approaching the intersection of Lewis and Glen Flora. Having just come from a meeting with one of his distributors that ran one of his big restaurants, Victor was in a great mood when he saw how smoothly business was going, and the delicious chicken tortas he had just eaten.

The gas light on his dashboard lit up as he came to the intersection. Victor cursed, never liking it when he had to get out of his vehicle in Waukegan.

At the intersection was a Jiffy Lube, a Popeye's Chicken, and a Mobil gas station. The light at the intersection turned yellow. He hit the gas, entering the left turn lane and banged his turn before it turned red, then swerved a right turn into the gas semi-crowded gas station, parking at a pump close towards the entrance doors to the store.

Hopping out in an expensive Salvatore Ferragamo suit, with an expensive *Roger Dubious* time piece on his wrist, Victor went to the pump and used his credit card to pay for the gas.

As he pumped, he noticed an older beat-up Chevy Trailblazer enter the gas station from the Glen Flora entrance, and at the same time, from the entrance at Lewis Ave, a rare big body BMW Alpina B7 entered.

Leaning against his Land Rover, he watched Trailblazer as it parked behind him. From behind the wheel, he saw a long-haired chick that was very skinny, hop out in a tight pink dress, with fishnet pantyhose on, and stilettos. Victor squinted his eyes at the body, then the face, and frowned, when he realized it was *not* a female.

He wrinkled his nose up at the cross-dressed homosexual, then looked at the BMW as it parked a few islands down from him.

Then windows were tinted all the way around. The driver door opened up, and out came a *stupendously* gorgeous woman get out.

The girl that was driving had delicious-looking light brown skin, golden-blonde hair, a gorgeously young and angelic face, and the tight painted-on jeans she had on made her ass look *sooooo* damn fat!

Now that is a woman! he thought to himself, feeling his dick hardening up.

She walked past him, not looking his way at all. Breaking his neck to watch her, his eyes traveled down to her big round booty. But then, he noticed the logo decaled on the back of her shirt.

Dedicated Transport, LLC! Wait! he thought, racking his brain. *I've seen her before...but where?*

Victor thought long and hard as the girl made her way to enter the store. The second she was inside, it hit him.

Shit! That's the Dominican's little sister!! he realized, as the memory of when his cop uncle showed him family photos of the Valdez family.

Hurrying up to finish gassing up his SUV, Victor capped his tank, then he grabbed his semi-automatic from inside his whip. He quickly tucked it into the rear of his pants waist line, fixed his suit jacket over it, then looking around, seeing that nobody was paying him any attention, he stepped off, hurrying towards the store's entrance, to catch up with the girl that held the key to making Javier Valdez surrender himself, or his baby sister was going to di*e.*

To Be Continued…

Lock Down Publications and Ca$h Presents
Assisted Publishing Packages

Due to an increase in the price of services we have increased our prices. The prices below reflect the price increase as of 11/1/24.

BASIC PACKAGE $699 Editing Cover Design Formatting	UPGRADED PACKAGE $1000 Typing Editing Cover Design Formatting Upload eBooks to Amazon Upload Paperback to Amazon
ADVANCE PACKAGE $1,400 Typing Editing (line editing/content) Cover Design Formatting Copyright Registration Proofreading Upload eBooks to Amazon Upload Paperback to Amazon	LDP SUPREME PACKAGE $1,700 Typing Editing (line editing/content) Cover Design Formatting Copyright Registration Proofreading Set up Amazon Account Upload eBooks to Amazon Upload Paperback to Amazon Advertise on LDP's Amazon and Facebook Page

***Other services available upon request.
Additional charges may apply

Lock Down Publications
P.O. Box 944
Stockbridge, GA 30281-9998
Phone: 470 303-9761
Email: lockdownpublications@gmail.com

163

Submission Guideline

Submit the first three chapters of your completed manuscript to ldpsubmissions@gmail.com. In the subject line add **Your Book's Title**. The manuscript must be in a Word Doc file and sent as an attachment. Document should be in Times New Roman, double spaced, and in size 12 font. Also, provide your synopsis and full contact information. If sending multiple submissions, they must each be in a separate email.

Have a story but no way to send it electronically? You can still submit to LDP/Ca$h Presents. Send in the first three chapters, written or typed, of your completed manuscript to:

LDP: Submissions Dept
P.O. Box 944
Stockbridge, GA 30281-9998

DO NOT send original manuscript. Must be a duplicate. Provide your synopsis and a cover letter containing your full contact information.

Thanks for considering LDP and Ca$h Presents.

NEW RELEASES

BLOODLINE OF A SAVAGE 1,2&3
THESE VICIOUS STREETS 1,2&3
RELENTLESS GOON
RELENTLESS GOON 2
BY PRINCE A. TAUHID

THE BUTTERFLY MAFIA 1-3
BY FUMIYA PAYNE

A THUG'S STREET PRINCESS 1,2&3
BY MEESHA

CITY OF SMOKE 1& 2
BY MOLOTTI

STEPPERS 1,2&3
THE REAL BADDIES OF CHI-RAQ
BY KING RIO

THE LANE 1&2
BY KEN-KEN SPENCE

THUG OF SPADES 1,2&3
LOVE IN THE TRENCHES 2
CORNER BOY CHRONICLES
BY COREY ROBINSON

TIL DEATH 3
BY ARYANNA

THE BIRTH OF A GANGSTER 4
BY DELMONT PLAYER

CHRISTOPHER "DIESEL" HORNEZES

PRODUCT OF THE STREETS 1&2
BY DEMOND "MONEY" ANDERSON

NO TIME FOR ERROR
BY KEESE

MONEY HUNGRY DEMONS 1,2&3
BY TRANAY ADAMS

HUNGRY FOR MONEY 1&2
BY SLIMBOS

A THUGGISH PASSION
KILLAZ ON STANDBY 1&2
LAND OF DA HOOLIGANZ 1,2&3
FRESH OFF DA PORCH
BY IRA B.

COUNTDOWN OF A KILLA 1&2
GUNS DOWN, BOTTOMS UP 1&2
SEX, MURDA AND GOD
BY LO-LIFE

THE LEVEL UP 1&2
BY LUXURY KING

FO'EVA ROLLIN' 1&2
BY ASSA RAYMOND BAKER

HUB CITY MENACE 1&2
BY J. WHITE

KILLA CREW
DYING FOR LIKES
BY ARYANNA

166

TIPPIN' THE SCALES

IF YOU CROSS ME ONCE 6
ANGEL 5
By Anthony Fields

IMMA DIE BOUT MINE 5
By Aryanna

A THUGS STREET PRINCESS 3
EMBRACING THE LOVE OF A BOSS
By Meesha

PRODUCT OF THE STREETS 3
By Demond Money Anderson

STANDING ON HER BUSINESS
BY DG SANTANA

GET IT IN SLUGS 1&2
B. STALLS

CORNER BOYS 2
By Corey Robinson

THE MURDER QUEENS 6&7
By Michael Gallon

CITY OF SMOKE 3
By Molotti

CONFESSIONS OF A DOPEBOY
By Nicholas Lock

TENDER
BY KHUFU

CHRISTOPHER "DIESEL" HORNEZES

THA TAKEOVER
By Keith Chandler

BETRAYAL OF A G 2
By Ray Vinci

CRIME BOSS 4
By Playa Ray

Coming Soon from Lock Down Publications/Ca$h Presents

RAN OFF ON THE PLUG 2 by **PAPER BOI RARI**
STREET REDEMPTION by **TONY DANIELS**
SAVAGE FAMILY EMPIRE by **PRINCE TAUHID**
BAD BITCHES WIT' GUNZ by **DIESEL**
THE SINGLE LADIES by **DIESEL**
COKE BY THE TRUCKLOAD by **DIESEL**
PROBLEM SOLVED by **DIESEL**
TIPPIN' THE SCALES by **DIESEL**
OPPS CRY TOO by **SAYNOMORE**
A GANGSTA'S KARMA by **FLAME**

AVAILABLE NOW

RESTRAINING ORDER 1 & 2
By **CA$H & Coffee**

LOVE KNOWS NO BOUNDARIES 1-3
By **Coffee**

RAISED AS A GOON I, II, III & IV
BRED BY THE SLUMS I, II, III
BLAST FOR ME I & II
ROTTEN TO THE CORE I II III
A BRONX TALE I, II, III
DUFFLE BAG CARTEL I II III IV V VI
HEARTLESS GOON I II III IV V
A SAVAGE DOPEBOY I II
DRUG LORDS I II III
CUTTHROAT MAFIA I II
KING OF THE TRENCHES
By **Ghost**

LAY IT DOWN I & II
LAST OF A DYING BREED I II
BLOOD STAINS OF A SHOTTA I & II III
By **Jamaica**

LOYAL TO THE GAME I II III
LIFE OF SIN I, II III
By **TJ & Jelissa**

IF LOVING HIM IS WRONG…I & II
LOVE ME EVEN WHEN IT HURTS I II III
By **Jelissa**

TIPPIN' THE SCALES

PUSH IT TO THE LIMIT
By **Bre' Hayes**

BLOODY COMMAS I & II
SKI MASK CARTEL I, II & III
KING OF NEW YORK I II, III IV V
RISE TO POWER I II III
COKE KINGS I II III IV V
BORN HEARTLESS I II III IV
KING OF THE TRAP I II
By **T.J. Edwards**

WHEN THE STREETS CLAP BACK I & II III
THE HEART OF A SAVAGE I II III IV
MONEY MAFIA I II
LOYAL TO THE SOIL I II III
By **Jibril Williams**

A DISTINGUISHED THUG STOLE MY HEART I - III
LOVE SHOULDN'T HURT I II III IV
RENEGADE BOYS 1-4
PAID IN KARMA 1-3
SAVAGE STORMS 1-3
AN UNFORESEEN LOVE 1-3
BABY, I'M WINTERTIME COLD 1-3
A THUG'S STREET PRINCESS 1&2
By **Meesha**

CUM FOR ME 1-8
An LDP Erotica Collaboration

BLOOD OF A BOSS 1-5
SHADOWS OF THE GAME
TRAP BASTARD
By **Askari**

CHRISTOPHER "DIESEL" HORNEZES

A GANGSTER'S CODE 1-3
A GANGSTER'S SYN 1-3
THE SAVAGE LIFE 1-3
CHAINED TO THE STREETS 1-3
BLOOD ON THE MONEY 1-3
A GANGSTA'S PAIN 1-3
BEAUTIFUL LIES AND UGLY TRUTHS
CHURCH IN THESE STREETS
By **J-Blunt**

THE STREETS BLEED MURDER 1-3
THE HEART OF A GANGSTA 1-3
By **Jerry Jackson**

WHEN A GOOD GIRL GOES BAD
By **Adrienne**

THE COST OF LOYALTY 1-3
By **Kweli**

BRIDE OF A HUSTLA 1-3
THE FETTI GIRLS 1-3
CORRUPTED BY A GANGSTA 1-4
BLINDED BY HIS LOVE
THE PRICE YOU PAY FOR LOVE 1-3
DOPE GIRL MAGIC 1-3
By **Destiny Skai**

A KINGPIN'S AMBITION
A KINGPIN'S AMBITION II
I MURDER FOR THE DOUGH
By **Ambitious**

A DOPEBOY'S PRAYER
By **Eddie "Wolf" Lee**

TIPPIN' THE SCALES

TRUE SAVAGE 1-7
DOPE BOY MAGIC 1-3
MIDNIGHT CARTEL 1-3
CITY OF KINGZ 1&2
NIGHTMARE ON SILENT AVE
THE PLUG OF LIL MEXICO 1&2
CLASSIC CITY
By **Chris Green**

LOVE & CHASIN' PAPER
By **Qay Crockett**

THE KING CARTEL 1-3
By **Frank Gresham**

THESE NIGGAS AIN'T LOYAL 1-3
By **Nikki Tee**

GANGSTA SHYT 1-3
By **CATO**

THE ULTIMATE BETRAYAL
By **Phoenix**

BOSS'N UP 1-3
By **Royal Nicole**

I LOVE YOU TO DEATH
By **Destiny J**

BROOKLYN HUSTLAZ
By **Boogsy Morina**

GANGSTA CITY
By **Teddy Duke**

173

CHRISTOPHER "DIESEL" HORNEZES

TO DIE IN VAIN
SINS OF A HUSTLA
By **ASAD**

I RIDE FOR MY HITTA
I STILL RIDE FOR MY HITTA
By **Misty Holt**

A GANGSTER'S REVENGE 1-4
THE BOSS MAN'S DAUGHTERS 1-5
A SAVAGE LOVE 1&2
BAE BELONGS TO ME 1&2
A HUSTLER'S DECEIT 1-3
WHAT BAD BITCHES DO 1-3
SOUL OF A MONSTER 1-3
KILL ZONE
A DOPE BOY'S QUEEN 1-3
TIL DEATH 1-3
IMMA DIE BOUT MINE 1-5
By **Aryanna**

BROOKLYN ON LOCK 1 & 2
By **Sonovia**

A DRUG KING AND HIS DIAMOND 1-3
A DOPEMAN'S RICHES
HER MAN, MINE'S TOO 1&2
CASH MONEY HO'S
THE WIFEY I USED TO BE 1&2
PRETTY GIRLS DO NASTY THINGS
By **Nicole Goosby**

THE STREETS ARE CALLING
By **Duquie Wilson**

TIPPIN' THE SCALES

LIPSTICK KILLAH 1-3
CRIME OF PASSION 1-3
FRIEND OR FOE 1-3
By **Mimi**

TRAPHOUSE KING 1-3
KINGPIN KILLAZ 1-3
STREET KINGS 1&2
PAID IN BLOOD 1&2
CARTEL KILLAZ 1-3
DOPE GODS 1&2
By **Hood Rich**

STEADY MOBBN' 1-3
THE STREETS STAINED MY SOUL 1-3
By **Marcellus Allen**

WHO SHOT YA 1-3
SON OF A DOPE FIEND 1-4
HEAVEN GOT A GHETTO 1&2
SKI MASK MONEY 1&2
By **Renta**

GORILLAZ IN THE BAY 1-4
TEARS OF A GANGSTA 1/&2
3X KRAZY 1&2
STRAIGHT BEAST MODE 1&2
By **DE'KARI**

TRIGGADALE 1-3
MURDA WAS THE CASE 1-3
By **Elijah R. Freeman**

MARRIED TO A BOSS 1-3
By **Destiny Skai & Chris Green**

CHRISTOPHER "DIESEL" HORNEZES

SLAUGHTER GANG 1-3
RUTHLESS HEART 1-3
By **Willie Slaughter**

GOD BLESS THE TRAPPERS 1-3
THESE SCANDALOUS STREETS 1-3
FEAR MY GANGSTA 1-5
THESE STREETS DON'T LOVE NOBODY 1-2
BURY ME A G 1-5
A GANGSTA'S EMPIRE 1-4
THE DOPEMAN'S BODYGAURD 1&2
THE REALEST KILLAZ 1-3
THE LAST OF THE OGS 1-3
By **Tranay Adams**

KINGZ OF THE GAME 1-7
CRIME BOSS 1-4
By **Playa Ray**

FUK SHYT
By **Blakk Diamond**

DON'T F#CK WITH MY HEART 1&2
By **Linnea**

ADDICTED TO THE DRAMA 1-3
IN THE ARM OF HIS BOSS
By **Jamila**

LOYALTY AIN'T PROMISED 1&2
By **Keith Williams**

FOREVER GANGSTA 1&2
GLOCKS ON SATIN SHEETS 1&2
By **Adrian Dulan**

TIPPIN' THE SCALES

YAYO 1-4
A SHOOTER'S AMBITION 1&2
BRED IN THE GAME
By **S. Allen**

TRAP GOD 1-3
RICH $AVAGE 1-3
MONEY IN THE GRAVE 1-3
CARTEL MONEY
By **Martell Troublesome Bolden**

TOE TAGZ 1-4
LEVELS TO THIS SHYT 1&2
IT'S JUST ME AND YOU
By **Ah'Million**

KINGPIN DREAMS 1-3
RAN OFF ON DA PLUG
By **Paper Boi Rari**

THE STREETS MADE ME 1-3
By **Larry D. Wright**

CONFESSIONS OF A GANGSTA 1-4
CONFESSIONS OF A JACKBOY 1-3
CONFESSIONS OF A HITMAN
By **Nicholas Lock**

I'M NOTHING WITHOUT HIS LOVE
SINS OF A THUG
TO THE THUG I LOVED BEFORE
A GANGSTA SAVED XMAS
IN A HUSTLER I TRUST
By **Monet Dragun**

CHRISTOPHER "DIESEL" HORNEZES

QUIET MONEY 1-3
THUG LIFE 1-3
EXTENDED CLIP 1&2
A GANGSTA'S PARADISE
By **Trai'Quan**

CAUGHT UP IN THE LIFE 1-3
THE STREETS NEVER LET GO 1-3
By **Robert Baptiste**

NEW TO THE GAME 1-3
MONEY, MURDER & MEMORIES 1-3
By **Malik D. Rice**

THE LIFE OF A HOOD STAR
By **Ca$h & Rashia Wilson**

THE STREETS WILL NEVER CLOSE 1-4
By **K'ajji**

LIFE OF A SAVAGE 1-4
A GANGSTA'S QUR'AN 1-4
MURDA SEASON 1-3
GANGLAND CARTEL 1-3
CHI'RAQ GANGSTAS 1-4
KILLERS ON ELM STREET 1-3
JACK BOYZ N DA BRONX 1-3
A DOPEBOY'S DREAM 1-3
JACK BOYS VS DOPE BOYS 1-3
COKE GIRLZ
COKE BOYS
SOSA GANG 1&2
BRONX SAVAGES
BODYMORE KINGPINS
BLOOD OF A GOON
By **Romell Tukes**

TIPPIN' THE SCALES

CREAM 2-3
THE STREETS WILL TALK
By **Yolanda Moore**

CONCRETE KILLA 1-3
VICIOUS LOYALTY 1-3
By **Kingpen**

THE ULTIMATE SACRIFICE 1-6
KHADIFI
IF YOU CROSS ME ONCE 1-5
ANGEL 1-4
IN THE BLINK OF AN EYE
By **Anthony Fields**

NIGHTMARES OF A HUSTLA 1-3
BLOOD AND GAMES 1&2
By **King Dream**

HARD AND RUTHLESS 1&2
MOB TOWN 251
THE BILLIONAIRE BENTLEYS 1-3
REAL G'S MOVE IN SILENCE
By **Von Diesel**

MOB TIES 1-7
SOUL OF A HUSTLER, HEART OF A KILLER 1-3
GORILLAZ IN THE TRENCHES
By **SayNoMore**

BODYMORE MURDERLAND 1-3
THE BIRTH OF A GANGSTER 1-4
By **Delmont Player**

FOR THE LOVE OF A BOSS 1&2
By **C. D. Blue**

CHRISTOPHER "DIESEL" HORNEZES

KILLA KOUNTY 1-5
By **Khufu**

MOBBED UP 1-4
THE BRICK MAN 1-5
THE COCAINE PRINCESS 1-10
STEPPERS 1-3
SUPER GREMLIN 1-4
By **King Rio**

MONEY GAME 1&2
By **Smoove Dolla**

A GANGSTA'S KARMA 1-4
By **FLAME**

KING OF THE TRENCHES 1-3
By **GHOST & TRANAY ADAMS**

QUEEN OF THE ZOO 1&2
By **Black Migo**

GRIMEY WAYS 1-3
BETRAYAL OF A G
By **Ray Vinci**

XMAS WITH AN ATL SHOOTER
By **Ca$h & Destiny Skai**

KING KILLA 1&2
By **Vincent "Vitto" Holloway**

BETRAYAL OF A THUG 1&2
By **Fre$h**

TIPPIN' THE SCALES

THE MURDER QUEENS 1-6
By **Michael Gallon**

FOR THE LOVE OF BLOOD 1-4
By **Jamel Mitchell**

HOOD CONSIGLIERE 1&2
NO TIME FOR ERROR
By **Keese**

PROTÉGÉ OF A LEGEND 1&2
LOVE IN THE TRENCHES 1&2
By **Corey Robinson**

THE PLUG'S RUTHLESS DAUGHTER 1&2
By **Tony Daniels**

BORN IN THE GRAVE 1-3
CRIME PAYS 1&2
By **Self Made Tay**

MOAN IN MY MOUTH
By **XTASY**

TORN BETWEEN A GANGSTER AND A
GENTLEMAN
By **J-BLUNT & Miss Kim**

HERE TODAY GONE TOMORROW 1&2
By **Fly Rock**

PILLOW PRINCESS
By **S. Hawkins**

SANCTIFIED AND HORNY
by **XTASY**

CHRISTOPHER "DIESEL" HORNEZES

WOMEN LIE MEN LIE 1-4
FIFTY SHADES OF SNOW 1-3
STACK BEFORE YOU SPLURGE
GIRLS FALL LIKE DOMINOES
NAÏVE TO THE STREETS
By **ROY MILLIGAN**

LOYALTY IS EVERYTHING 1-3
CITY OF SMOKE 1&2
By **Molotti**

THE BUTTERFLY MAFIA 1-4
SALUTE MY SAVAGERY 1&2
By **Fumiya Payne**

THE LANE 1&2
By **Ken-Ken Spence**

THE PUSSY TRAP 1-5
By **Nene Capri**

DIRTY DNA
By **Blaque**

BOOKS BY LDP'S CEO, CA$H

TRUST IN NO MAN
TRUST IN NO MAN 2
TRUST IN NO MAN 3
BONDED BY BLOOD
SHORTY GOT A THUG
THUGS CRY
THUGS CRY 2
THUGS CRY 3
TRUST NO BITCH
TRUST NO BITCH 2
TRUST NO BITCH 3
TIL MY CASKET DROPS
RESTRAINING ORDER
RESTRAINING ORDER 2
IN LOVE WITH A CONVICT
LIFE OF A HOOD STAR
XMAS WITH AN ATL SHOOTER

www.ingramcontent.com/pod-product-compliance
Lightning Source LLC
Chambersburg PA
CBHW071214260626
47162CB00004B/1287